A Cinderella Retelling

DISDAIN

A Tale of Cinder
Book 2

M.J. HAAG

ISBN 978-1-943051-21-2 (eBook Edition)
ISBN 978-1-943051-53-3 (CreateSpace Paperback Edition)
ISBN 978-1-943051-23-6 (Paperback Edition)

The characters and events in this book are fictitious. Any similar to real persons, living or dead, is coincidental and not intended by the author.

Editing by Ulva Eldridge
Cover design by Shattered Glass Publishing LLC

To Catherine for helping shape an amazing person. I know she misses you every day.
To my sprint group, Heather, Meg, and Chanda. Thank you for keeping me accountable and on track! I promise I'll be back soon.

DISDAIN

A single blow shattered my life of glass. They shouldn't have left me with the shards.

Eloise knows the name of her mother's murderer, but she cannot speak it. A curse keeps her silent and locked in the tattered remains of her once charming life. Though magic holds her tongue, it doesn't quell the smoldering spark of her anger or her need to learn the reason behind her mother's death.

However, games of magic have dire consequences. Desperate to keep those she loves safe from the repercussions of her actions, Eloise must make a bold gamble with her safety and virtue that could win her everything or destroy her forever.

Two lives hang in the balance. For, if Cinder fails, Snow will fall, too.

CHAPTER ONE

I LAY BEATEN AND CHAINED TO THE HEARTH, ANGER MY ONLY companion as the events that led me to this circumstance vividly replayed in my mind. I'd been so blind to who was responsible for the murder of my family, and that ignorance had cost me far too much. I would not allow Maeve to take any more from me.

A stab of agony shot through my face when I clenched my teeth at the thought of the woman who'd killed my mother. Maeve would pay. I'd find a way. Somehow.

The sound of the door opening stilled my tormented thoughts.

"You will need to prepare dinner tomorrow for a small group. Ten, perhaps. Something suitable to be served in a fine home."

"Yes, My Lady," Heather and Catherine said.

The sound of Maeve's voice enflamed my anger anew.

Keeping my eyes closed, I forced myself to push the emotion aside so I could think logically.

Maeve was planning on serving dinner to guests. How could I use that to my advantage? Since I couldn't speak out against Maeve because of the spell or show myself to whoever might be due for dinner because of the damned chain around my wrist, there was little I could do.

A whisper of sound was the only hint of Maeve's approach.

"Stand, Eloise."

"I cannot. It hurts to move," I said.

"Stand, or I will call Hugh so your sister can feel what you feel."

Slowly, I turned my head and looked up at Maeve. One of my eyes no longer fully opened, but I could see her well enough. She watched me fight the pain that stabbed across my middle as I set my hand on the floor and began to lift myself. I let all the anger I felt show in my eyes as I leveraged myself onto all fours. It took another few moments to gain my feet and slowly straighten.

Behind Maeve, I saw that Kellen worked alongside Heather and Catherine. All three kept their gazes downcast. However, despite my recent beating and the agony ripping through me at being forced upright, I was far from submissive.

"Why?" I asked Maeve.

"Why what, Eloise?"

A small smile curved Maeve's lips when I opened my mouth and choked on my words.

"When you find your voice, I'll answer your questions. Until then, walk around and exercise your legs. I expect you and your sister present and in good form for dinner tomorrow." She stepped closer to me. "Appearances, Eloise. Don't forget. I should hate for Kellen to suffer for your ineptitude."

If Maeve was so concerned about appearances, why would she want me to attend a dinner with my face so obviously marred? It didn't benefit me to question her, though. I wanted others to see me as I was because, even if I couldn't condemn her for it, they would know it happened under her care.

She turned to the others.

"Have a list ready for Hugh first thing in the morning. He will fetch whatever is needed. I have accounts to look through. When dinner is ready, I'll take it in the sitting room."

She glanced at me once more then departed.

Kellen rushed to my side and wrapped a supportive arm around me. I grunted at the contact. I felt certain something was permanently damaged inside of me. It shouldn't have hurt so much to breathe.

"I need a chamber pot," I said, my words as broken as I felt.

Catherine fetched it for me, and Kellen lifted my skirts to help me use it. She gasped at the sight of my legs. I didn't look. I didn't want to know. When I tried to squat, I groaned in pain.

"How will you ever sit through a dinner?" Kellen asked softly.

Her question echoed my own thoughts. It would be hell, but I would endure it to spare Kellen the same fate I currently suffered.

After dinner, Catherine and Heather retreated to their room; and Maeve came to return Kellen to our room until morning.

"And Eloise?" Kellen asked.

"Eloise has yet to understand that there are worse fates than to be a pampered daughter of a merchant. She will sleep where she is tonight."

The stone hearth was hard, but the fire kept the chill at bay. Twice I woke to drink the tea that Kellen had left for me. All in hopes that rest would help the healing. However, when the sun rose, I felt each injury more deeply, not less so.

Catherine and Heather moved about quietly, neither speaking to me as I slowly rose to my feet. Breathing continued to hurt, as well as using the chamber pot. When I finished, Catherine set a washbasin on one of the stools near the fire and took away the pot.

I glanced down at the water. My cheek was colorfully swollen just below my eye, which was why opening it had been difficult. Between that and the dirt marring my face, I looked like I lived a very rough life. Given all that had happened, it felt an accurate portrayal.

Picking up the cloth that Catherine had left, I washed carefully.

The door to the kitchen opened, and Hugh walked in with his arms full of firewood. He didn't look at me as he filled the bin. When he finished stacking all of the pieces, he went to the table and sat. Catherine glanced at him then me. An unnamed emotion crossed her expression before it disappeared again.

"We're fixing hot oats," she said. "It will be a few more minutes."

While they cooked and he stared at the wall, I started walking in slow circles. My chain rattled occasionally and tugged at my wrist. The discomfort was nothing compared to everything else.

Kellen entered the kitchen just as Heather placed the bowls on the table. Maeve was a step behind my sister.

"We will sit together," Maeve said, taking her place at the head of the table. Catherine hastily handed me my oats and went to join the others.

"Do you have the supply list for Hugh?" Maeve asked. She blew on her oats and took a tentative first bite.

Catherine and Heather cast nervous glances at each other before Heather answered.

"Yes, ma'am. Will dove served with fall roots and a brandy-berry sauce suit you?"

"It sounds lovely. Make sure it tastes so."

Sitting on the stool by the fire, I ate my oats and stared at Maeve. I hated her and still wanted to demand answers for questions I was forbidden to speak. My inability to do so only made my rage fester.

"Kellen, once you're finished, you will return to your room." Maeve looked at me. "Eloise, I suggest you remove the loathing from your expression when you look at me, or I will take your eyes."

She said it so calmly and in such a gentle voice that I didn't doubt her promise. Exhaling slowly, I masked what I felt for her.

"Much better," she said. "I will not tolerate that look from you again. Am I clear, Eloise?"

"Yes."

"Now, there is much to do today; and the more you move before dinner, the better you will feel. Once Kellen is safely locked in her room, you will assist Heather and Catherine then bathe and dress for tonight's guests. If you do anything other than that, your sister will suffer."

As she said the word suffer, her necklace glowed, and Kellen hissed out a breath and dropped her spoon.

"Do you understand me, Eloise?" Maeve asked.

"Yes."

"Very good. Now finish your meal. You need your strength."

IN THE ENTRY, I stood beside Kellen. Maeve's gaze swept over us, lingering on our hair and fancy mourning dresses.

While the need to attire ourselves so formally worried me, I couldn't bring myself to hate what I wore. The snug lacings made it a bit easier to breath and move.

"Well done, girls," she said, her voice echoing with true praise, which I knew to be false.

She reached into her pocket and produced a small, dark vial which she held out to me.

"Drink it all. It will mask the unfortunate state of your face for several hours."

I took the vial and uncorked it. I could feel Kellen stiffen beside me. I knew it wasn't wise to drink anything from Maeve. However, it was less wise to disobey her. She'd proven that.

Tipping back my head, I drained the vial and shivered at the taste of the contents. A moment later, my face tingled.

"Much better," Maeve said.

I glanced at Kellen and noted a flicker of shock in her expression as she stared at my face. I touched my cheek, gingerly testing the puffy flesh. It still pained me greatly.

"You're no longer bruised," Kellen said.

Before I could question her, carriage wheels crunched against stone outside.

"Just in time," Maeve said. She gave us one last sweeping appraisal before meeting our gazes. "Do not be misled into believing the presence of guests will protect you from any transgressions. The punishments will only be that much worse for you and those who bear witness. Do you understand?"

Kellen and I both nodded. We understood very well what was at risk. Yet, I was free from the chain, and Kellen was free from her room. If a moment presented itself, we would run.

When Maeve turned her back to us, Kellen's hand slipped into mine, and she gave me a light squeeze. My sister would be ready this time. I knew it in my heart.

Maeve opened the door to a quartet of finely dressed gentlemen.

"Lady Grimmoire," the first one said with a dashing bow and a kiss to the back of her hand. "I was quite pleased when my wife returned from her visit with an invitation to sup with you in a week's time. Although, I must say I'm curious as to the reason why."

"All will be explained in good time," Maeve said. "Come. Let us retreat to the dining room. The fire will warm us as will the brandy." She turned to Kellen and me. "Please lead the way, Eloise. Kellen and I will wait for the remaining three guests to join us."

Kellen discreetly released my hand, and I led the way to the dining room. The men helped themselves to glasses of brandy then tried to enquire why they were invited without their wives.

"Is it a business proposition?" one asked.

"I'm sorry. I don't know."

"It must be business. Why else would we be here?" another asked.

Now that I knew what she'd done to my family, I could think of only one reason for her invitation. Yet, these were men of note. People who would be missed if they disappeared. Certainly, Maeve couldn't mean to kill them. Especially not when she'd invited them a week ago before our attempted escape and my beating. If not to kill them, why invite them at all? What purpose could they serve for her?

It wasn't long before Kellen and Maeve joined us with three other well-dressed men.

"Gentlemen, please have a seat," Maeve said. She looked at me then Kellen and motioned for us to sit to her right and left. I sat gingerly while the men took the remaining chairs.

"Thank you all for joining us this evening. Let us eat first and speak of business matters afterward," Maeve said.

The door to the kitchen opened, and Catherine and Heather emerged with covered platters. They began placing them before the men, making several trips to ensure everyone had a plate.

Maeve raised her glass.

"To new connections and power," she said. The men around the table brightened and returned her toast then lifted the lids from their platters.

Under the table, Kellen nudged me, and I hurried to unveil my meal. The little fowl sat prettily on a bed of sliced roots. The brandy-berry sauce glazed the crisp skin and had my mouth watering. I took my first bite, expecting delight only to embrace the pain of chewing. I kept my bland yet proper expression carefully in place and forced myself to keep going.

There was some light conversation around the table while we ate. It wasn't until I heard a familiar name that I fully paid any attention.

"Alliances aren't just for the Royal Houses," one man said.

"Agreed," another said. "Alliances for those of us in business are just as important. We must protect our interests in these dangerous times."

"Dangerous times?" Maeve asked.

"Yes. I suppose you don't hear much out here. But a Mrs. Tiller and her niece were found dead in their separate homes. Honest working women, the both of them."

Kellen briefly met my gaze then focused on her meal. I did the same, struggling to keep the anger and hate off my face.

"That's unfortunate," Maeve said. "Such deaths are unnecessary. But the topic of alliances does bring me to my purpose for inviting you here."

The men set down their forks and gave Maeve their full attention. From the corner of my eye, I caught movement in her amulet and kicked Kellen under the table. She glanced at me, and I closed my eyes, hoping she would do the same. I didn't know how Maeve's magic worked, but she'd asked me to look at her when she'd cursed me. I had no intention of being cursed again.

"I struggle to build my power with the paltry offerings in this secluded area," Maeve said, her chair scraping against the floor. "I'm inviting you to join me as I create an influence over this tired town. If you give your consent to help me in whatever small ways you can, I can offer you my support in return, along with limitless pleasure away from the censure of your wives."

One of the men at the table groaned his agreement. Then another. One by one they succumbed to whatever spell Maeve was casting.

"Girls, open your eyes," Maeve said.

I reluctantly did and saw the men had their gazes fixed on us. Panic bloomed in my chest as one reached under the table to stroke his groin.

"Catherine. Heather," Maeve called.

The door to the kitchen opened, and Heather and Catherine emerged fully nude. Shock and decency had my gaze locked on Catherine's face. She wore an expression of hopelessness.

"I believe Mr. Wineford would like his cock sucked," Maeve said, pointing to the man next to me.

Catherine came to his side, helping him loosen his trousers, and got to her knees. I quickly looked at Maeve, surely she didn't mean for—

The onset of wet slurps from Catherine and heated groans from the man made my face flush scarlet.

"Heather, choose one," Maeve said, gesturing to the remaining men.

Heather moved to another man and did the same as Catherine.

Two threads of green rose into the air and floated toward Maeve's necklace. A satisfied smile curled her lips as she looked at me.

"Tell me, Eloise. Do you wish to lead the life of a serving wench or that of a proper young lady?"

CHAPTER TWO

"I wish to lead the life of a proper young lady," I said demurely.

"I thought as much. Kellen, Eloise, come with me."

I quickly fled my seat, keeping my gaze fixed on the wall as I joined Maeve near the kitchen door. Despite my focus, I still glimpsed what was happening to poor Catherine and Heather.

The men were crowding around them, touching them. One man had lifted Catherine's hips so her backside was in the air. While she continued to service the first man with her mouth, the second man stood behind her with his pants around his ankles. He began to thrust into her vigorously.

My face heated further. Though I wished to save Heather and Catherine, I could do nothing unless I wanted to join them.

Kellen's fingers brushed against mine. Maeve's smile only grew at the gesture. She opened the door and waved for us to enter the kitchen. Another green thread joined the first two, and even as the door closed, it touched the amulet.

"Take off your dress," Maeve said, looking at me.

Panic took flight in my chest.

"Please, Maeve," Kellen begged softly. "Eloise won't—"

"I do not intend to send her to those men. Catherine and Heather will suit their needs well enough. Now remove the dress, Eloise. I will not repeat myself again."

With shaking fingers, I undid the row of buttons along the bodice then the ribbons underneath. The dress slid down my torso, and I carefully stepped out of the skirts. Standing in just my underthings, I clutched the mass of material to my chest.

Maeve held out her hand. Reluctantly, I surrendered the garment.

"Put the cuff around your wrist," Maeve said.

Relieved that I was only being chained to the fireplace, I did as she said. Once the metal clicked back into place, Maeve gave me a pleased smile.

"Very good, Eloise. You've done well today. I'm proud of the effort you've made. Perhaps in a few days we won't need the chains, and you'll be able to rest with your sister in the comfort of your own room. Wouldn't that be nice?"

I nodded, and Maeve looked at Kellen.

"Come, Kellen. Time to put you to bed. Perhaps tonight you won't mind the lock on your door."

"Thank you," Kellen said softly, giving me one last look before following Maeve from the room.

Though my body still ached, my mind was clear. I sat on the stool near the fire and stared into the flames, considering what I'd learned this evening while trying not to hear the sounds coming from the dining room. Pieces fell into place. The way the amulet glowed when Maeve used its power. The threads of green that came from the men. Whatever was happening in the dining room was a dangerous magic. I felt certain that Maeve was draining the men as a means to power her amulet. Why? And why now?

A week ago or more, Maeve had invited these men into our home. Was the outcome of this dinner her intent all along? Was that why she'd killed Judith and Anne? So she could bring two whores here to suit her purpose? I remembered Maeve's reaction to Heather and Catherine, though, and struggled with what was real and what had been pretense. She hadn't known I would overhear her slapping Hugh, had she? I felt certain her anger had been real. Would she have used any maid Hugh had found in such a manner? Or, the more chilling thought, would she have used Kellen and me if maids hadn't been found? Maeve wasn't above hurting us. My current state proved that. Yet, she hadn't let the men touch us tonight. Why? More importantly, why did she need more power?

I thought of the way the men's pleasure had fed the amulet. What was she planning to do with the power she collected? Nothing good. That much was obvious.

Rubbing my hand over my face, I tiredly reached for the cold tea still sitting by the stool and drained the contents. It was the same tea I'd used to send Hugh into a deeper sleep, and I hoped it would help me tonight. However, as I lay on the hearth waiting for sleep to claim me, I heard every grunt and masculine laugh from the adjoining room. My heart hurt for Heather and Catherine. They'd thought they'd escaped a life of whoring by coming here.

I wasn't sure how long I lay there drowsing before the sounds finally began to quiet.

The door separating the kitchen from the dining room opened, and I scrambled to my feet in a panic, almost passing out with the pain in my side. It wasn't any of the men entering the kitchen, though. Only Catherine and Heather, still nude and now flushed, both carrying stacks of plates.

Neither one would look at me.

"I'm so sorry," I said softly.

"Don't be," Catherine said. "You tried to warn us. It wasn't so bad."

She set her plates on the block and started back for the dining room.

"They weren't mean," Heather assured me. "It could have been much worse. Would it bother you if we bathed?"

"Not at all."

Outside, carriage wheels scraped against stone as our guests departed.

While Catherine collected the rest of the dishes, I moved the tub before the hearth, and Heather hauled water. They didn't even wait for it to warm before bathing. I sat on the stool and watched the flames, giving them what privacy I could.

Once they finished, they emptied the tub and started washing the dishes.

Tired and numb from the day and the pain of my still aching limbs, I lay down before the hearth once more. I was just dozing off when something brushed against me. I looked up at Catherine as she covered me with one of their blankets.

"Will you get in trouble for this?" I asked.

"I don't think so."

"I truly am sorry. I wish I could have done something."

Catherine shook her head.

"You made the right choice. I would have done the same."

She lightly brushed her fingers over my bruised cheek and left me.

I was sitting on the stool by the fire when Kellen and Maeve joined us in the kitchen the next morning.

"Very well done last night, girls," Maeve said.

She sat at the table, and Catherine hurried to set a soft-boiled egg and a plate of fresh biscuits before her.

"Thank you, Catherine." Maeve used her spoon to crack into her egg. "I expect we will have more company of the female variety today. Please make sure to have a tea tray ready and some of those delightful pastries."

She finished her meal without a glance at me then left the room. As soon as she did, Kellen rushed to my side. Without a word, she hugged me tightly. It hurt my side and my face, but I didn't utter a sound. I couldn't. Not when she was shaking so badly.

"I thought she was going to make you go to them."

"Shh..." I said, stroking her hair. "I know. But, she didn't. It's all right."

"I'm so sorry, Eloise."

"There's nothing to be sorry for. None of this is your fault. You know that."

There was a scrape of noise behind us. I lifted my head and found Catherine cleaning up the table.

"I'm going to go walk the pig," Heather said.

"I'll go feed the chickens," Catherine said.

I studied their guilt-laced expressions as they left, slightly confused.

"They have ears," Kellen said, easing her embrace. "And mouths to repeat what they hear, whether they want to or not."

Then, I understood. They'd left so we could have a private word. I wouldn't waste the opportunity.

"You need to leave," I said. "Find a way to run."

"No. She promised she would—" Kellen winced and rubbed her throat.

"I don't think she will," I said, understanding what she couldn't say. "Maeve has had the opportunity and hasn't done anything. Instead, she's used my safety to control you. And yours to control me. Why, Kellen? Why would she want to control someone she intends—?" I winced when my throat clenched.

"She wouldn't." Kellen frowned. "Why does she need us controlled?"

The door behind her swung open, and Maeve looked at the pair of us on the floor.

"You need something to occupy your time, Kellen. Speaking to your sister of things you shouldn't will only cause you pain. It's time we start clearing your father's room. Come."

Kellen gave my hand a squeeze and rose to follow Maeve.

I stared after the pair, my mind racing. How had Maeve known of what we spoke? Perhaps she'd overheard us on her way in. Or perhaps there was something more to her knowing.

I studied the chain and touched the metal plate again, feeling the zing of magic. Magic Maeve had created. Could she be connected to it still?

Grabbing the chain, I gave a strong tug. The links clanked and scraped against the loop, but the plate didn't budge. I picked up the fire poker and tried prying at the plate to no avail.

I pretended to be tending the fire when the outside door opened and Catherine entered. She didn't comment on the poker I returned to the holder. While she started making a new batch of pastries, I struggled with what to do with myself. Tethered as I was, I couldn't offer my help. And given last night's events, any conversation filled with idle pleasantries would be inappropriate. I couldn't pretend it hadn't happened and didn't want her to either.

With nothing pleasant to discuss, I walked small circles, doing what I could to ease my aches. When I grew tired of that, I asked Catherine if she would make me some tea so I could rest. It helped me sleep well for a few hours, and I woke before lunch to listen as Catherine and Heather made small meat pies for each of us.

From my position on the floor, I stared at the flames and considered the plight of those within our home. I could do nothing to help any of us. And locked in her room at night or under Maeve's watchful eye during the day, Kellen was just as much of a prisoner as I.

While Heather and Catherine were free to come and go, they couldn't speak of Maeve's wrongdoings any more than Kellen or I could. Even if they could, though, I doubted they would speak out against Maeve. They feared her too much.

That meant, if Kellen and I were to be free again, we would need to free ourselves. However, even if one of us found a way to escape, how would we be able to rally help to save the other when we couldn't speak of what had happened?

I stuck my finger into the ash near the hearth and attempted to write "Maeve killed my mother" in the soot. As soon as I started the M, my throat squeezed uncomfortably. I ignored it and fought through the increasing discomfort to shape the second mountain of the M. Writing the letter "A" proved harder as breathing became difficult. Wheezing, I managed her full name before collapsing to the floor. The force strangling my airway didn't immediately ease, and I clawed at my throat.

Heather looked up from her pies, noticing my silent struggle.

"Eloise?" She rushed to my side and tried helping me to sit up. By the time I was upright, I could gasp in a breath. Then another. Slowly the pain eased.

"What happened?" she asked.

Behind her, Catherine stared at me with wide eyes. Moving my hand as if to better brace my weight, I wiped away the evidence of my attempt.

"Nothing more than my own stupidity," I rasped. "I'm sorry for startling you."

"Can I get you some more tea?" Catherine asked.

I shook my head.

"Some water would be better."

She nodded and quickly fetched some. I took a few tentative sips, wincing as I swallowed. My throat felt bruised. After watching me take several swallows, the pair went back to work preparing our midday meal.

I set aside the question of how we would rally help once one of us escaped and focused instead on thinking of a safe haven. Kellen and I had no other family or friends to turn to. Where could two women go?

"If you could travel anywhere, where would you go?" I asked Catherine and Heather.

Catherine frowned and gave it thought while Heather snorted.

"It does no good to dream of a better life," she said. "Best get used to the one you have because while your mind is wandering, your life could become much worse."

"There's no harm in dreaming. It helps pass time when things aren't pleasant," Catherine said, giving me an understanding smile. "I think I would like to see the south. I hear it's warm, even in the winter, and women wear gowns so thin you can see their skin through them. But they aren't considered whores for that display of flesh. Men treat them like sought after objects to be protected and revered."

Both Heather and I gave Catherine skeptical looks. The woman shrugged a shoulder.

"I'm not saying I believe it. Only that I'd like to travel there to see if it is true."

"I think the only truth to that story is that the south is warm."

"Where would you go, Eloise?" Catherine asked.

I turned to gaze at the fire.

"There's no point of dreaming of going anywhere when I'm chained," I said softly.

After that, they worked in silence until the kitchen door opened and Maeve walked in. She gave me a long hard look.

"What did Eloise do while I was gone?" she asked the pair.

"She moved around a bit then asked for tea to help her sleep. When she woke, she choked a bit but recovered," Catherine said.

"And she asked us where we would go if we could go anywhere," Heather added.

"Oh? And where would Eloise go?" Maeve asked, studying me.

"She said there was no point in her dreaming of going anywhere when she's chained," Catherine said.

Maeve's lips curled.

"Exactly why you wear the chains," she said softly. "I suggest you stop testing the limits of my spell. You might find yourself with Judith and Anne if you don't."

I nodded jerkily.

"Good. Let's eat," she said cheerfully. "Kellen and I have worked up an appetite."

Catherine and Heather served everyone before joining

Kellen and Maeve at the table. Maeve had barely eaten more than a few bites when the sound of a carriage rattling up our drive filled the kitchen. She made a sound of annoyance and set her fork aside.

"Do not leave Kellen and Eloise unattended," she said to Catherine and Heather. Then, she pinned Kellen with a cold gaze. "If you try to run, your sister will suffer. Do you understand?"

Kellen nodded quickly.

Maeve swept out of the kitchen, and Kellen quickly stood with her plate and joined me by the fire.

"Are you all right?" she asked.

"As well as I can be. Why?" I looked down at the bruises visible on my arms and legs.

"I was with her when the—" She immediately stopped and touched her throat then her hand slid lower, resting just above her breast. She watched me steadily, and I knew she wanted me to understand something. It dawned on me when I looked at her chest again.

She'd seen Maeve's amulet glow when I tried writing Maeve's name in the soot. That meant Maeve was still connected to the spell. She would know any time either of us tried to speak against her or, in my case, write against her. That made the possibility of escaping to find help even more unlikely. Maeve would know any time we plotted.

I frowned and reconsidered. Perhaps not. The curse hadn't flared when I thought of running and finding help.

It had only let Maeve know when I had tried to speak or write anything to implicate her of wrongdoing.

Catherine picked up the tea tray she'd hastily put together for the unexpected visitors and left the kitchen.

"She forgot the cream," Kellen said, standing. "I'll go get it."

While she descended into the cold storage, I continued eating. Heather started washing the dishes. A thought struck me, and I reached out once more to write in the soot.

You must run.

I wrote the message without a hint of pain. Relief swept through me, and I picked up my plate, slowly eating.

Kellen returned with the cream a few moments later and set the container on the table just as Catherine returned for it.

"Thank you," Catherine said before rushing out of the room once more.

Heather, with her back to us, didn't see me point to the fireplace as Kellen joined me. Nor did she see Kellen shake her head.

I wiped the message clean with my left hand and wrote a new one.

We need help.

I lifted my wrist, showing her the cuff binding me. She reached out and touched my bruised face then every additional bruise she could see. I understood what she was saying. Maeve would likely beat me again.

Wiping the message clean, I wrote the only thing I could think of to convince her.

Without you, there is no control.

Kellen stared at my words for a long time.

"Are you two finished?" Heather said, glancing back at us.

"Almost," I said. "The crust on this meat pie is delicious. Is there more?"

Heather smiled slightly, obviously pleased with the compliment.

"I'm sorry, miss. We only made the six. When Catherine returns, she is going to take Hugh his portion."

"Let him eat oats," Kellen said, her eyes darkening. "He deserves nothing more."

Heather's expression showed her conflict.

"It's fine, Heather," I said. "Give Hugh his portion. I know where the blame for his actions truly lies."

Heather nodded and turned back to her wash water.

Kellen sighed.

"Fine. You will have your way."

To Heather it would sound like she was agreeing to let Hugh have his portion. But I knew better. She was agreeing to run.

Heart aching, I reached out and wiped away the soot. There had never been a time in my life when I'd been without my sister. Not like what I was proposing.

Kellen took my empty plate from me and sat on the stool. I leaned my head against her thigh, missing her already. Her fingers stroked through my hair, her gentle touch lulling me. We stayed like that for a long while. I shifted occasionally but remained close to her. This was our goodbye. Kellen had committed to finding us help, and she would discover a way to escape.

The sound of a carriage outside was the only warning we had before the door opened, and Maeve strode in.

"Kellen, I would like to continue clearing your father's room. Come," Maeve said. Kellen immediately stood and went to Maeve, who studied me closely.

"You're covered in soot, Eloise."

I glanced down at myself, only seeing the soot on my hand. Still, I wiped at my face with the unsoiled hand and tried to remove the soot from the dirty one by scrubbing it against the cleaner stones near the hearth. It only made the mess worse.

"Fetch the ash bucket for Eloise. She can clean the fireplace since she's covered in soot," Maeve said, looking at Heather before addressing me once more. "Perhaps next time you will find a way to stay cleaner."

I did my best to look suitably chastised as Maeve turned and left the room with Kellen in tow. On the inside, grief shredded me, and I wondered if I would ever see her again.

"Here are the buckets, miss," Heather said. "Put the cold ash in the empty one and use the other to wash away the soot."

I worked for hours cleaning the stone around the fire.

Each time the water dirtied, one of the two maids would empty it and return with fresh water. When I finished, my arms ached from scrubbing, but the hearth looked as clean as I'd ever seen it. I, however, had never been filthier.

Without a word, Catherine hauled out the tub and started filling it with water.

CHAPTER THREE

"Hugh!" Maeve's yell echoed throughout the house.

I bolted upright from my place beside the hearth and looked at Heather and Catherine who were already quietly cooking the morning meal.

"What's happened?" I asked groggily.

"I don't know, miss," Catherine said, wiping her hands and rushing from the room.

While Catherine was unsure, I had no doubt what had caused Maeve's yell. Kellen had escaped. My heart pounded with excitement, hope, and fear.

After dinner last night, Kellen had helped me comb and braid my hair. With Maeve's permission, she'd also made me an extra strong batch of tea to help me sleep through the night. I'd known why Kellen had wanted me to sleep soundly and had thanked my sister. However, while

Kellen hoped the tea would spare me, I knew the tea wouldn't stop what was to come.

"Are you hungry, miss?" Heather asked. "We have oats ready."

"Thank you, Heather. I think I'll use the chamber pot first."

I managed to empty my bladder and wash before Maeve entered the kitchen, Catherine in tow.

"Where is she?" Maeve asked.

I frowned and glanced at Catherine as if confused.

"Your sister," Catherine said.

Maeve reached out and slapped the woman.

"She knows very well of whom I speak. Keep your mouth closed unless I tell you to open it. Go fetch Hugh."

Catherine nodded and scurried for the outer door.

"I don't know where Kellen is," I said before Maeve could ask again.

Maeve stalked forward, anger lighting her gaze. I could feel the crackle of power that surrounded her.

"Do not lie to me, child. Every word you speak to me will be the truth."

The amulet at her neck glowed and an unnatural warmth wrapped around me, squeezing my skin before seeping inside.

"Now, where is your sister?" Maeve asked again.

The power wormed through me, nesting in my throat and coating my tongue.

"I don't know," I answered, relieved Kellen and I hadn't discussed where she would go.

Maeve's eyes narrowed.

"You knew she was going to run."

I remained silent.

"Tell me everything you told her yesterday."

"I told her I was all right."

"Omission is a lie," Maeve said, and her power surged again.

I was compelled to speak but still chose my own words.

"I told her to run. That you were using her to control me."

The kitchen door opened, and Hugh walked in, Catherine close at his heels. He didn't seem to notice. His gaze locked on Maeve and never wavered.

"I want you to hurt Eloise," she said. "And continue hurting her until she tells me everything."

Before I could say I had told her everything, Hugh pivoted and hit me. Pain exploded in my face, knocking me back. Robbed of breath from the first blow, I couldn't even make a sound when his foot connected with my already bruised thigh.

My mouth opened in silent agony. Hugh rained down blow after blow—arms, legs, ribs—showing me that I'd barely scraped the level of hell to which my life could descend with my first beating. However, unlike the first time, I remained conscious.

When he stopped, panting from his exertion, I lay

limply on the floor. My pulse throbbed through my body, and I struggled to think beyond the agony I felt.

"Tell me everything," Maeve said softly. "What did you say?"

I coughed a laugh, too hurt to care that such a move might provoke her or that it sent another wave of pain through me.

"I said nothing. I wrote in the soot." It hurt to form those simple words with my bruised lips. "Told her to run. You control me through her." I shifted my gaze to look at Maeve, a slow smile curving my lips despite the pain. "Wise to chain me."

Rage filled Maeve's eyes. Her face flushed, and her hands fisted as she stared at me.

"Shall I hurt her more, Maeve?" Hugh asked.

Unconsciousness would be a blessing. Instead, she exhaled slowly and regained control.

"No. Our Eloise has nothing more to tell us. Go to town and find the best tracker you can. Bring him here quickly. Do not disappoint me, Hugh."

Hugh nodded and left.

"Look after Eloise," Maeve said. "If any ill fate claims her because of her punishment, the same will befall you."

As soon as she swept out of the room, Catherine and Heather both moved with speed. Heather ran outside, and Catherine grabbed the tub. I closed my eyes and drifted for a bit until strong arms gripped me.

"This will hurt, miss," Catherine said.

Suddenly I was lowered into a frigid bath. I groaned weakly and tried to lift myself out.

"Not yet, miss," Heather said. "Take a breath and go under. Let the water ease your pain."

I blinked at her, wondering if she was encouraging me to drown myself.

"Big breath," Catherine said.

I only had a moment to breathe shallowly before she pushed me under. The cold water soothed my throbbing face. Submerged, I realized most of my aches were benefiting from the treatment.

Hands tugged at me, and I emerged from the water gasping.

"Another big breath," Catherine said a moment before she eased me back under.

My vision swirled as I looked up from the water. Flames danced with shadows and faces above me. It was quiet and peaceful where I was, and I tiredly wished I could stay. The cold welcomed me, and the small inhale I'd taken escaped on a sigh.

They pulled me up quickly, and I feebly inhaled. Closing my eyes, I waited for whatever would come next, no longer caring.

"She can't rest on the stone," one of the pair said.

"I'll fetch my mattress," the other said.

Arms pulled me from the tub and back onto the floor. Each move sent more waves of pain through me, but I began to feel disconnected from it. Darkness bled through my vision, closing around me in a comforting embrace of nothingness. I welcomed it.

A pungent smell pierced my nose and jerked me back into awareness.

"You cannot sleep, Eloise," a voice said. "I know you're tired, but you must focus."

I blinked, unsure if I wanted to do what was asked of me. The beat of my heart echoed in my swollen face, aching arms, and bruised legs. Focusing meant acknowledging there wasn't a part of my body that didn't hurt.

"Think of your sister," another voice said softly. "She needs you."

The image of Kellen's face swam in my mind. My promise never to leave her had me trying to look around. The fire. The tub. Catherine and Heather's worried expressions as they hovered over me. I remembered it all.

"Yes," I said. "Kellen."

"That's a good girl," Heather said. "We need to sit you up and fill you with some tea. It's something I made. It will keep you awake and help with the pain."

I gave the barest nod, wincing with the movement.

Heather slid her arm under my shoulders, leveraging me up as Catherine pressed a cup to my lips. I drank everything, each swallow more painful than the last. My stomach wanted to rebel, and I clasped Heather's arm when she would have lowered me. She moved behind me, letting me rest against her, and smoothed her hand over the top of my head.

"Fate can be fickle and cruel," she said softly. "But it's up to you whether to fight or accept what it hands you."

I thought of what it had handed me. Death. Brutality. Captivity. I refused to accept that would be the remainder of my life. Kellen had escaped. She would come for me and I needed to be ready.

"I'll fight," I said raggedly.

Catherine watched me from her place on the stool. I could see the fear in her eyes that I wouldn't have the strength to continue to live. Fear that she and Heather would be doomed to a fate similar to mine.

"Run," I said. "Like Kellen. Before you die."

Catherine looked at Heather. Heather's hand stilled on my head for only a moment before continuing.

"We've been in positions like this before, with clients who liked to hurt us. It will pass," Heather said softly.

I reached up and gripped her arm.

"It won't."

"It will. Kellen won't leave you here. She'll bring help," Catherine said. "We'll be fine until then."

I closed my eyes and sighed. My insides tingled oddly, and I realized some of the pain was fading. It made breathing easier.

"Feeling better?" Heather asked.

"Yes." The fire was warming my feet, but I shivered lightly in my wet shift. "Can I have dry clothes?"

"Not yet. You need to go back into the cold bath again. It will help the bruising and the pain. Ready to sit up?"

The bath was more shocking the second time. I shivered in the water and dunked down when told. When I reemerged, Heather had a towel waiting for me. I rubbed away what moisture I could and sat on the stool, wincing as the wood pressed against the bruised backs of my legs.

Catherine stood behind me, combing through my hair with gentle strokes.

Before my hair fully dried, the thunder of horse hooves rang out in the yard. Catherine and Heather, who had started fixing the midday meal, halted. It wasn't until that moment that I recalled Hugh had gone to town for a tracker. I thought of my sister and her inability to recognize an animal print in the dirt. Would she know to walk on firm ground? Would she know not to break branches? I frowned further, wondering if she would know to disguise herself while in town.

We listened to Hugh call out in the main entry.

"Continue cooking," I said to Heather and Catherine. "Whatever happens, Maeve will still expect a meal."

They started moving again but continued casting nervous glances at the door separating the kitchen from the dining room.

We didn't have to wait long before Maeve swept in with a man following her. He was large and well-muscled, his skin weathered from the outdoors. The dirty cap sat askew on his head with deep-brown unwashed hair poking out haphazardly.

His dark eyes swept over the room, barely hesitating on me or the manacle chaining me to the fireplace. The corners of his mouth turned down slightly though, and that gave me hope. Perhaps he would—

"This is Kellen's sister, Eloise," Maeve said. "When you find Kellen, be sure to describe in detail how Eloise appears now."

"Do you know where the girl might be headed?" the man asked, killing my hope.

Maeve glanced at me before shaking her head. Hugh, who'd entered behind the man, stepped forward.

"I suspect she will go to town. They know nothing else but this estate and Towdown."

Hugh's betrayal hurt even though I knew his willingness to help Maeve was due to a spell.

"We need Kellen found quickly and returned," Maeve said.

"There are many places to hide in Towdown," the tracker said.

"I have the means to help you find her." She withdrew a ribbon from her pocket. The vibrant red color was unmistakable. Kellen's ribbon.

"Heather, empty one of the spice boxes."

Heather turned to the shelves beyond the block and plucked a large spice box from the shelf. It held one of the more common herbs from our garden, which she dumped onto the block.

I watched Heather hand the small chest to Maeve and wondered what Maeve meant to do. The amulet around her neck began to glow as she opened the box and placed the ribbon inside.

"Treasure divided. Treasure made whole. Let what's lost be found. Let what's taken be returned."

A hum filled the air, and the wooden box began to pulse with a faint light. The glow from the necklace grew brighter with each word.

"If you should lose Kellen's trail, hold the box in your hands and command it to show you the way to Kellen. Its magic will guide you but at a cost. Each time you use it, you will age a year."

His gaze flicked to the box, but there was no fear, only curiosity.

"It shouldn't take me long then. I'll return with her soon."

"You will be rewarded if you do," she said. "But before returning, check the ribbon in the box. If the ribbon is whole, bring the girl to me alive."

"Unharmed?" he asked.

Maeve's gaze flicked to me.

"A few bruises will not concern me."

The man nodded his understanding.

"And if the ribbon does not stay whole?" he asked.

Maeve's lips curled into a smile that made my insides

shiver.

"If the ribbon withers and fades into dust, cut the girl's heart out of her breast and place it in the box. Do you understand?"

"Yes, My Lady."

He bowed his head and left the room. Maeve looked at Hugh.

"Go back into town and extend an invitation to my partners. Let them know they can bring a friend if they so choose." Hugh nodded and quietly let himself out.

Maeve came to me, bending down so we were level. The pendant swung freely, now a dull green.

"I control whether the ribbon remains whole or turns to dust. If you cause trouble, the tracker will kill your sister. Do you understand, Eloise?"

I nodded, and the manacle around my wrist fell free.

"Help Heather and Catherine in the kitchen. If the meal is not ready on time, they will suffer the next beating. Do you understand, Eloise?" she repeated.

My loathing for the woman deepened.

"And do you know what will happen if you try to run?" she said softly.

"I will kill them all slowly, draining them of life as the blood leaves their bodies from a thousand small cuts. And when I find you again, you will bathe in it."

Unable to help myself, I shivered because I believed every word.

"I understand," I said, my voice rough.

"Good. And hope, for the sake of all the innocent people of Towdown, that Kellen hasn't done something to cause me ill fortune." She straightened and looked at the maids. "You can thank Kellen and Eloise for tonight's gathering and the power I need to replenish. Prepare the meal for fifteen guests," she said before sweeping out of the room.

I looked at Catherine and Heather in horror, understanding what Kellen and I had condemned them to. They shared a look, and Catherine sighed.

"I'm so sorry," I rasped.

"Don't be. There are worse things than making fancy dinners and sucking on weathered old cocks."

"Really?" That sounded pretty horrible to me.

"Swallowing a bit of cum ain't so bad," Heather said. "Better than a busted rib."

I nodded and slowly stood, too afraid to ask what cum was.

"How can I help?" I took a step toward the block and almost collapsed. Although the pain was better, my strength had vanished.

"Sit on the mattress and rest," Catherine said.

Not arguing, I gingerly lowered myself to the soft bed. Exhaustion tugged at me, but my eyes refused to close. Instead of resting, I watched the pair move around the kitchen. Soon, the aroma of cooking meat filled the air. Heather brought me a bowl of mash which I slowly ate.

After that, I lounged on the mattress and thought of

where Kellen might be and the magic box Maeve had given the tracker. With such a tool in his hands, the man was sure to find Kellen quickly. And, despite Maeve's words, I hoped that Kellen had already spoken to many people and found help. I didn't want anyone to die, but neither did I want to perish myself. Perhaps if enough people knew, Maeve would be forced to end her game—whatever it might be— before attaining her goal. I deeply feared what goal would drive a person to the depths of wickedness to which Maeve had descended.

The carriages started arriving just after dark.

Men's voices rose from the dining room, a jolly gathering, for they knew what awaited them this time. Heather and Catherine hurried to serve the dishes then returned to the kitchen to clean up what they could. When they finished, they stripped out of their gowns and waited near the door.

Anger tore at me. Self-loathing for being able to do nothing. Fury that Maeve was forcing Catherine and Heather to do what they'd come here to cease doing.

"I will find a way to stop her, I promise," I said softly.

"You mustn't speak like that," Catherine said quickly, looking upset.

"Especially not to us. Do you understand?"

I studied their worried expressions and nodded. Too well, I remembered the compulsion to tell Maeve everything.

"You're right. It's best to accept my place in life," I said.

"I'll rest and heal so I can help you in the kitchen as best as I can."

Maeve called their names, and Catherine gave me a fleeting smile before they walked out the door. With the tea still numbing me from the pain and keeping me wide awake, I slowly moved around the kitchen. I couldn't do much. My strength eluded me, and I knew that running wouldn't be an option even if I wasn't concerned about Kellen, Catherine, and Heather.

In the dining room, the laughter became more subdued, replaced with the growing sound of groaning and panting. I returned to my bed and covered my ears, laying thusly for what seemed like half the night before things quieted.

When the kitchen door opened, Heather and Catherine shuffled in. They looked tired as they carried dishes to the wash bin. I sat up, feeling the aches and bruises more acutely now.

"Let me get the dishes while you wash," I said.

They nodded and moved toward the door.

"Do you want to dress first?" I asked, unsure if they were aware they would be walking out into the yard naked.

"No," Heather said wearily. "We would only dirty our clothes."

It was then that I noticed the odd sheen to their skin in certain places.

"A girl can only swallow so much cum," Catherine said.

"If cum baths made a woman look young, I bet the wives of these men would never let them leave home."

The pair chuckled as they left. I didn't see what was so funny.

Limping my way to the dining room, I started gathering dishes. It took me a long while as I had to stop frequently to breathe and brace myself against the table. My legs started throbbing with increasing pain by the time I made it into the kitchen with the first stack of plates.

Heather and Catherine weren't yet back, so I returned to the dining room for more dishes.

Maeve walked in, the amulet around her neck once more a vibrant green. She paused at the sight of me.

"What are you doing?" she asked.

"Clearing the table while Heather and Catherine bathe."

She sighed as if exasperated with me.

"Eloise, this work is beneath you."

I frowned.

"But you told them to make sure I worked. I thought you wanted—"

"I want you to learn your place," she said. "Something you seem to have difficulty doing."

I said nothing. I didn't know if this was some new game or if there was something I truly wasn't understanding. More than anything, I wished Kellen was here. Not in pain or captivity with me, but to guide me. She was the smart one who could see things clearly. Not me.

Maeve continued to study me. The final stack of plates grew so heavy in my abused arms that I started to shake. Her lips curled slightly when she saw it.

"I think you might be learning, Eloise. Return those to the kitchen, then rest. Heather and Catherine will clean the rest of this."

She didn't need to ask if I understood, but I nodded automatically as if she had. Her smile widened further, and in that moment, I truly did understand. My place was under her thumb. Under her control. And, she was starting to believe she had me there.

She turned and left the room, and I stared after her, keeping my expression impassive. I'd let her think she was training me. My goal hadn't changed. I would find a way to stop her. Even if the tracker returned with my sister, I would find a way.

Maeve will suffer all that I suffer, I vowed silently.

CHAPTER FOUR

I SAT CAREFULLY ON THE BENCH BESIDE CATHERINE.

"You should be resting," Heather said, watching me.

"I will lose more strength if I lie about all day. I'm better if I move around."

"Trust us," Catherine said. "Rest heals faster than forcing yourself to move about."

The door swung open, and Maeve walked in with a large smile on her face. Catherine immediately rose to fetch Maeve's breakfast.

"Today is the day," she said, joining us at the table.

My heart stopped for a moment as fear clawed its way up my throat.

"Kellen?" I asked before I could stop myself.

Maeve's expression soured for a moment before it cleared and she continued to crack open her egg.

"Your ungrateful sister and the tracker remain

unaccounted for. However, that will soon change. My things arrive today." Her gaze swept over me in scrutiny. "Take a proper bath and put on an appropriate dress. Be ready within the hour." She finished her egg and left the room.

"Come," Heather said. "We'll help you wash."

I was ready to crawl into bed by the time we were done but knew I couldn't. With Heather's assistance, I dressed in one of my mourning gowns. The tight lacing made breathing less painful, and the tea Catherine once again made me drink alleviated most of the other aches. By the time I left the kitchen, I felt almost normal. However, like so many other things in my life, that was only an illusion.

The swelling in my cheek had increased overnight, making it difficult to fully open my eye. It served as a reminder that, although the pain was gone and I was once again dressed, I was far from the old Eloise.

Maeve paced the length of the foyer twice before noticing my presence. When she did, she stopped moving and studied me. A kind and caring smile lit her face.

"You look lovely, Eloise. A picture of refined beauty."

My stomach twisted at her words delivered with such sincerity. Did she truly think bruised and swollen was a picture of beauty? If so, I feared what Kellen's and my future would hold.

"I'm so nervous," she said. "It's been so long. Well over six months since I last saw them."

"Them?"

She ignored me and went to the door.

"It feels as if a piece of myself is finally returning. As if I'm about to be whole again."

That I could understand. Since Kellen left, it felt like a piece of myself was missing, too.

Maeve checked her reflection in the foyer mirror and met my gaze in the glass.

"So many things will change once the wagons get here. But your place won't. Do you understand, Eloise? You will remain important to me. Always."

I nodded. Like her previous statement, there was a scary truth lacing her words. How and why was I important to her? Was I only another sacrifice, or was I something more? I was about to give voice to my first question when the sound of several conveyances rumbling into the yard caught my attention.

Maeve's gaze swung to the door, and with giddy enthusiasm, she moved to open it. I trailed in her wake as she stepped outside.

A carriage pulled to a stop in front of the door. Behind it, three loaded wagons did the same. Before I could try to guess what all the oilcloth wrapped objects might be, the carriage door burst open, and a young woman dressed in a fine green gown emerged.

"Mama!" she shouted with joy as she ran at Maeve. Maeve caught her up in a tight hug. The girl's light brown hair swung slightly with the impact. Petite and slightly rounded, the girl didn't look much like her mother. It gave me hope.

"I've missed you, my darling Porcia," Maeve said softly.

She lifted her head and looked over her daughter's shoulders at the second young woman exiting the carriage. This one looked much more like Maeve with her tall, slender figure. However, where Maeve was dark, this one was golden, like me. She smiled at Maeve and gave her a more discreet hug.

"Hello, Mama," she said.

"Hello, my sweet Cecilia."

The three separated and turned to where I waited on the stairs.

"Girls, I would like to introduce you to one of your new stepsisters," Maeve said.

My breath caught, and I fought not to stare at Maeve in horror. How could I have forgotten? Father had married this monster, giving her more power over me than a set of chains.

"This is Eloise. Eloise, these are your new sisters, Porcia and Cecilia."

Cecilia smiled at me serenely as she came and gave me a firm hug. I involuntarily gasped at the pain that speared my rib cage. She loosened her hold. However, instead of asking if I was all right, she pulled back and placed a kiss on my swollen cheek. Had I been uninjured, it would have felt like a true welcome. However, since she chose to kiss me right where the swelling was the worst, I knew she was just like her mother.

She released me and stepped back for Porcia to embrace me. The younger girl's hold wasn't as tight as her sister's, but it still created an ache in my ribs despite the tea. When she kissed me, she chose the same spot as her sister, though.

"It warms my heart to see you girls welcome Eloise to our family." Maeve smiled at us then looked over the wagons.

"Is everything in order?" she asked.

"It is, Mama," Cecilia said. The girl motioned to the men who had been sitting in their seats staring straight ahead. At her signal, they climbed down from their perches and started untying the ropes securing the items in the wagon beds.

"Come inside, girls," Maeve said. "I'm sure you're ready for tea and a seat that doesn't jostle you."

Maeve left the door open behind us as we made our way into the house. The first man followed us inside, carrying in a small table which he set in the foyer before I entered the dining room.

"Catherine," Maeve called.

Catherine came straight away.

"Yes, Lady Grimmoire?"

"Tea please. And biscuits if you have them."

"Yes, ma'am." Her gaze never once flicked to me as she turned and disappeared into the kitchen once more.

"I have a room cleared for one of you," Maeve said. "The other still needs attention."

I'd never asked Kellen what they were doing in Father's room. But it made sense now, that Maeve would want it cleared so she could sleep there. I hated that any of them would be sleeping in mother's room. Even my new sisters.

"I'm sure the men outside will be happy to help us," Cecilia said.

"Very good. Now tell me about your journey. Was there any trouble?"

"None. We were very selective about our drivers. They've served us well along the way."

Maeve beamed at her daughters.

"It's so good to be together again. I hated leaving you behind."

"It was necessary," Porcia said. "We understood."

Catherine arrived with a tea tray and biscuits.

"Eloise, will you pour for us?" Maeve asked.

It was the task of a hostess to serve, one I didn't mind performing under normal circumstances. As it was, it hurt to stand, pour, then reach with cups extended. But I was sure Maeve knew that. They all accepted their tea with words of thanks and kind smiles. When I sat, I took a moment to catch my breath. They waited, watching me.

"Serve yourself, dear, so we can start," Maeve said gently.

No matter what tone she used, it was an order. My hand

shook with exhaustion as I poured my cup and placed a biscuit on my plate.

"Well done, dear," she said. She sipped her tea and glanced out the door.

"Would you like me to tell the men to unload it straight away?" Cecilia asked.

"No. That's not necessary. It's only good to hear its call again. I didn't realize how much I missed it."

I kept my eyes fixed on my tea, taking a small sip while retaining the calm, relaxed expression I'd kept since the night before. It didn't surprise me that Maeve could hear something I couldn't. Whatever called to her was likely magical in nature, and likely just as deadly as her necklace.

They finished their tea in silence while I focused on the footfalls of the men as they came and went with pieces of furniture.

"Come, girls. It's time to show you your new home."

Maeve rose as did her daughters. Since I already knew this home, I remained seated. Maeve's gaze swung to me.

"You're one of my girls too, Eloise. Never doubt that. Come along."

I stood and followed on shaky legs. Perhaps when Maeve finally let me return to the kitchen, I would ask for another cold bath.

Maeve showed her daughters the sitting room, Father's small study which was rarely used, and the kitchen where Heather and Catherine were working to prepare the midday meal. After that, Maeve led us upstairs. There weren't that many steps, but each one brought a new level of agony. Twice, I had to stop to breathe. Maeve turned to watch me, waiting until I reached the top before continuing.

"This will be your room, Cecilia," Maeve said. "I know it will be snug, but you will fit in it better than your sister."

Cecilia's smile sharpened a little, and her gaze darted to Porcia who watched her toes.

"Do you see something interesting down there?" Maeve asked.

The girl's gaze immediately snapped up to her mother's.

"No, Mama."

"Good. Would you like to see where you will sleep?"

The girl nodded and smiled. We followed Maeve toward Mother's room. However, she didn't stop at that door. She continued to the room I shared with Kellen and opened the door.

"As I said, it still needs to be cleaned out. Perhaps you should start on that while Cecilia and I direct the men."

"Yes, Mama," Porcia said, looking a little pale.

"Very good. Come along Cecilia and Eloise." Maeve turned and walked away. I lingered a moment, staring longingly at my bed.

"She's waiting," Porcia said softly.

When I met her eyes, there was no pity or kindness there.

Turning, I limped toward the stairway where Maeve and Cecilia did indeed wait.

"I apologize for keeping you," I said.

"My," said Cecilia. "You do speak. I'm ever so grateful you're not a mute. I'm looking forward to having another sister with whom I can speak."

"As am I," I said serenely.

Cecilia's smile deepened.

"Come. I'm anxious to set our household to rights," Maeve said. She glided down the stairs and started looking at the pieces waiting to be carried upstairs.

Cecilia quirked a brow at me and executed the same graceful descent. When she reached the bottom, she turned. I smiled, ignoring the pain in my face, and smoothly moved down the steps. Slowly. Cecilia turned to her mother when I reached the bottom.

"I fear I packed it too well, and it may take them some time to unload it. Do you mind if I borrow one of the men to start setting up my room?"

"Not at all, dear. Keep an eye on your sister and ensure she's making progress in her room."

"Yes, Mother."

Cecilia nodded and walked out the door.

Despite the men moving in and out of the room, it felt as though I'd suddenly been left alone with Maeve. The long wooden rod from a wardrobe rested against the stair railing. My fingers itched to pick it up and bash the woman over her head. My uncertainty of successfully killing her stopped me from attempting it.

"What are you thinking, Eloise?" she asked.

I could feel the compulsion to answer and almost let my shock show. Catching myself just in time, I smiled serenely, already having learned it was what she expected.

"That I'm not strong enough in my current state. And I'm sorry for it."

She studied me for a moment then held out her hand. I accepted it, acting the part she wanted me to play.

"Sweet child, it pains me to see you unhappy. Let us agree never to argue again."

Did she truly believe that was what had happened? There'd been no arguing. Only her killing and subsequent commands to hurt me.

"Yes, Maeve," I said.

"Mama," she corrected.

I couldn't. I wouldn't. She would never be my mother.

She watched me intently, and I saw the moment an angry light started to grow in her eyes. She reached up to her necklace, stroking the stone with her free hand.

It's an act, I reminded myself. *Nothing this woman does or says has any true meaning.* To keep my sister safe, I would play her game.

"Yes, Mama," I said softly.

"It pleases me to hear you say that. Go now. Check on the midday meal, and rest until it's ready." I wanted to ask her where she expected me to rest but caught the knowing look in her eyes.

"Yes, Mama." She released me, seemingly satisfied with my mock obedience.

I went to the kitchen and found Catherine and Heather sitting at the table, just waiting. They reminded me of the wagon drivers, and that worried me.

"Maeve—" Remembering their warning about what I said to them, I started again. "Mama asked that I come in here and check on the midday meal then rest."

Catherine and Heather exchanged a look.

"Mama?" Heather asked.

"She showed me a marriage certificate she and my father both signed before he left." I faced the fire quickly, hiding my face as the events before Maeve's arrival fell into place. Father's indifference regarding Mother's passing. His need to leave immediately. His choice to go to the Dark Forest. None of it had been him. Somehow, Maeve controlled him. She hadn't only killed one of my parents. She'd wanted to kill both. Why? Why kill both of them and not Kellen or me?

I shook with rage. Maeve had ripped apart my world, and I needed to learn why.

"Sit, miss," Heather said softly. "Try to rest as she wanted. Things will be better for you if you listen."

I nodded, knowing she was right and that she was only trying to protect me from an additional beating. Yet, I struggled to be calm enough to do as she suggested. I wanted to prowl the expanse of the kitchen and plot all the ways I could bring suffering to Maeve.

"It's here!" Maeve's voice rang out. "Cecilia, Porcia, Eloise."

Summoned, I had no choice but to answer.

I left the kitchen, my anger seething behind my carefully composed façade. In the main entry, Maeve stood before a wrapped object. As tall as she and twice as wide, the flat piece leaned against a wall.

Porcia and Cecilia made their way down the stairs and reached their mother before me. I watched Maeve reverently run her hand down the oilcloth.

"You've come so far," she said softly. "Faithful, true, and unbreakable. The one thing on which I can always depend."

I glanced at Porcia and Cecilia from under my lashes, but neither seemed bothered by their mother's affection for an inanimate object.

Maeve cut the thin ropes holding the oilcloth in place and slowly drew the covering off. Underneath, a clouded panel of glass reflected our murky images. Its thick wood frame bore evidence of extravagant workmanship. Carved decorative swirls merged with images of animals and plants. It should have been a thing of beauty. Yet, my stomach twisted while looking at it.

"There you are," Maeve said softly. "How I've longed for you."

She leaned forward and pressed her lips against the glass.

"We are pleased to reunite you, Mama," Cecilia said.

Maeve smiled lovingly at her daughter's reflection then ran her hands along the frame.

"Mirror, Mirror against the wall, I summon you now to answer my call. Show me Kellen."

The glass shimmered gold then green, our reflections fading as a new image developed. Through the dimly lit trees, my sister ran as if being chased. The cloak of her dark hood had fallen back, showing her pale skin and ebony braid.

"Show me the tracker," Maeve said. The image shifted to the man Maeve had sent after my sister. He sat upon a horse that trotted through trees.

"Good," Maeve said, glancing at me. "Our family will be together again soon."

"Yes, Mama," I said with a smile I truly felt. Not that I thought for a moment Kellen would be home soon. Wherever she had been wasn't where the tracker was. The lighting had been different along with the size of the trees. While I was relieved the tracker wasn't near her, I was also concerned. Why was Kellen running?

"Show me Prince Greydon," Maeve said.

I frowned slightly and watched the image of the tracker fade. Nothing replaced the man's craggy face and worn mount, however. The glass darkened, showing nothing but a wall of black.

Maeve's smile faded. Cecilia reached out and pressed her sister back while retreating a step herself. I quickly did the same.

Maeve's scream of rage startled me, but not as much as when she whirled around, her eyes wildly searching. I swallowed hard, expecting to feel the hand of her wrath. Instead, she moved to grab the same wooden rod I had considered, then took to beating the mirror. The rod didn't shatter the surface. The glass and wood remained unmarked even after enduring several minutes of Maeve's anger.

Maeve stopped just as suddenly as she'd started, tossed the rod aside, and smoothed back her hair. Her gaze swept over the three of us.

"I apologize, my darlings. It would seem our prince still hides behind his charm." She took another calming breath. "I must ask for your patience a bit longer."

"And that is something we will unfailingly give, Mama," Cecilia said.

"We know everything you're doing is for us all," Porcia said.

Maeve nodded and looked at the mirror again.

"Mirror, show me who Kellen spoke to since leaving this house."

The image of Mr. Bentwell materialized on the glass. He sat at his desk, reading an old looking book, as he often did. The image shifted back to its original grey.

"Mirror, mirror against the wall, from my presence you may now withdraw."

Maeve turned to us and smiled serenely once more.

"I know you've only just arrived, my dears, but it would seem we have urgent business in town. Eloise, it would be best if you stay here for the time being. We will return with news."

Maeve started toward the door, and Cecilia and Porcia hurried to follow. The sound of the carriage moving outside only moments later bespoke Maeve's urgency.

Leaving the men to finish carrying things upstairs, I returned to the kitchen.

"Please tell Lady Grimmoire that the meal will be ready shortly," Heather said, already dishing portions of a light stew onto plates.

"There is no need," I said dully. "Mama just left."

"Left?" Catherine asked, straightening from her artfully stacked pastry plate. "To go where?"

I opened my mouth to speak, but the words "To kill Mr. Bentwell" stuck in my throat.

After all, one didn't speak out against Mama.

CHAPTER FIVE

I ATE A QUIET MEAL WITH CATHERINE AND HEATHER. BY THE time I finished, all I could feel was the pulsing ache from my bruises.

"Is there anything that would help me heal faster than the tea?" I asked Catherine.

"Only rest and time, miss. The body will heal at its own pace."

I sighed and nodded. Her mattress still waited by the fire for me.

Surprisingly, the world drifted away easily when I closed my eyes. I didn't know how long I slept before Heather gently shook me awake.

"They've returned. Perhaps you should meet them at the door."

I nodded groggily and managed to stand without hurting myself too much. I'd just made it to the foyer when the door opened and the three women walked in speaking animatedly as women often did when returning from an outing. Most, however, didn't return covered in blood. However, the sight of their blood-spattered bodices and stained skirts didn't shock me as much as it should have.

"Eloise, my sweet," Maeve said. "I'm so glad you're here. We have a bit of a puzzle for you to solve."

"Yes, Mama," I said dutifully.

She held out her hand, and Porcia passed the book I hadn't noticed her carrying.

"It would seem Kellen, that sweet girl, only wanted to return a book and asked that Mr. Bentwell set aside a special one for you. She asked for it by title. Why would she want you to read this?" Maeve asked, handing the book to me.

I read the unfamiliar title then opened the book, leafing through the pages.

"I already thought to look for a message," Maeve said. "The book is unmarked with no notes hidden within its pages."

I looked up and let my confusion show.

"I don't know, Mama. I'm not familiar with this book and don't recall Kellen ever reading it, either."

"Read it. There's a reason she wanted you to. Solve the puzzle, Eloise."

"Yes, Mama," I said, hugging the book to my chest. "Are you hungry? Catherine and Heather have kept your plates warm."

"We ate while we were in town," Maeve said. Her lips curled in that way that made my blood run cold and my stomach twist as I saw the evidence of Mr. Bentwell's death with new eyes. Surely they didn't eat the man.

"Please tell the maids I would like a bath in my chambers," Cecilia said.

"Me, too," Porcia added.

"There's only the one tub. It's very large and doesn't easily fit in the rooms. We typically bathe in the kitchen."

Cecilia's eyes narrowed, and I glanced at Maeve, unsure what was expected of me.

"Everything is well, my loves. We knew when we came here we would live rustically for a time. A bath before a crackling fire is quite enjoyable."

"Of course, Mama," Cecilia said, her annoyance smoothing out.

"Yes, Mama," Porcia said just as serenely.

The pair moved off in the direction of the kitchen, and Maeve held out her hand.

"Come, child. Let's read together."

Except for Maeve and me, the rest of the house had long since gone to bed. I rubbed my good eye, tired beyond compare, painfully shifted positions in my well-cushioned seat, and continued reading by the light of a candle.

Under Maeve's watchful gaze, I'd already read the

majority of the book and still had no idea why my sister had requested it for me. Not that I was actually trying to understand why. If Kellen was being secretive about a message, then she didn't want Maeve to know. If I didn't know, then Maeve couldn't compel me to tell her.

Stifling yet another yawn, I turned the page and felt immediate relief that I was almost to the end. I didn't know how Kellen could stay up half the night purposely reading. While I most certainly enjoyed a good tale, I enjoyed sleep more.

When I finished the last words, I looked up at Maeve.

"If there is a hidden meaning in these pages, it escapes me," I said honestly. "It's a book of fables and fairy tales. Perhaps she thought it was something I might enjoy reading?"

Maeve stood and knelt before me.

"Your sister saw me beat you and knew that I would beat you again if she ran. Why would she risk your health to return a book and ask for another on your behalf? Do not pretend to be simple, Eloise." She gently smoothed back a bit of my hair. "It will not end well for you."

"I'm not simple, Mama," I said, holding her gaze, "but neither am I as smart as Kellen. Perhaps she thought I would understand, but she overestimated me."

Maeve considered me for a moment.

"Your sister knows you too well. If she thought you would understand, you will." She stood, taking the book from me. "Go rest. You'll read it again when you wake."

"Yes, Mama," I said, stiffly getting to my feet. She followed me to the kitchen and watched me gingerly lower myself, fully dressed, to the mattress beside the fire.

"This is no place for a well-bred girl to rest," she said. "Tomorrow, we will change your accommodations."

"Thank you, Mama," I said tiredly, not meaning a word of it.

"Good night, my sweet."

I fell into sleep's waiting arms before the door closed behind her.

The slight scuffle of sound as Catherine and Heather worked to prepare the morning meal didn't fully rouse me. Neither did Maeve or my dear stepsisters when they ate in the dining room. I dozed in that blissful space between awake and asleep until Catherine said my name.

"Do you think Eloise is all right? She's been sleeping a long time."

"She's healing, and Maeve kept her up late." The way Heather said Maeve's name was the first indication she'd ever given that she might hate the woman more than she feared her.

"I heard. I wonder what it is about that book."

"Don't wonder. Work. If we do as we're told, maybe we'll live long enough to go back to whoring."

"I hate whoring."

"Did you see the state of these dresses I'm washing? I think there are worse things than whoring."

They fell silent, and I lay there in guilt. A guilt that I

knew I shouldn't feel but did regardless. If only they'd run when I told them. They could have been safely away. Then I realized that, even if they'd run, Maeve would have eventually gone after them for even knowing a hint of what she was doing. Just like Mrs. Tiller and Sabine. Just like Mr. Bentwell.

I shivered slightly and pulled the light blanket more closely around my shoulders.

"Miss, are you hungry?" Catherine asked.

Rolling over, I yawned and nodded. It took some time to sit up and then stand. Everything was stiff and sore. But slightly less so than the day before. And my eye could open more fully.

Catherine set a cloth-covered plate on the table.

"Would you like a warm salt bath?" Heather asked. "It will help with the remaining swelling and stiffness."

"That sounds lovely." I started to sit.

"Lady Grimmoire asked that we let her know once you're awake and fed," Catherine said.

I paused and looked at Heather then Catherine.

"I think I should perhaps bathe first?" They both nodded, and I smiled. They were trying to help me while still obeying Maeve. Although I appreciated their concern, I knew they were walking a fine line and hoped their kindness wouldn't get them in trouble.

Leaving the plate where it was, I moved to help Catherine and Heather.

"No, miss," Heather said. "Lady Grimmoire has made it

clear to us you're not here as kitchen help. You're her daughter and should be treated as such." I didn't miss the way her gaze swept over my bruises or the doubt in her expression when she said the word daughter.

Choosing not to sit, I walked around the kitchen to work out what aches I could and watched Heather and Catherine fill the tub. They'd already had water boiling, so it didn't take long before I was floating in a warm salt water bath.

"This should help your recovery," Heather said, patting my shoulder after the final bucket of hot water was poured. With my hair piled up on the top of my head, I sunk deeper, letting the water lap at my chin. The heat seeped into my flesh, soothing me. It felt lovely and relaxing. I would have liked to stay in the water until it turned cold, but I knew lingering too long would bring Maeve's wrath down upon Heather and Catherine.

With reluctance, I pulled myself from the tub the moment the water lost its heated sting. Catherine was there with a towel for drying and a cream for the deeper bruises along my ribs.

"I'm not sure this will help," she said. "But it won't hurt."

"Thank you."

As soon as I was dressed, I grabbed my biscuit.

"I'll go to Mama with you."

I didn't want Catherine to face Maeve alone. Based on the angle of light coming through the kitchen window, I felt certain that Maeve and her daughters had eaten breakfast several hours ago.

Catherine gave me a grateful smile and led the way out of the kitchen. We found Maeve in the sitting room at the writing desk. She looked up as we walked in.

"Eloise, you are not a street urchin. You do not eat and walk but sit at a table like a refined person."

I quickly swallowed the bite of biscuit I had in my mouth and guiltily glanced down at the remains before meeting Maeve's gaze.

"I'm sorry, Mama. I slept longer than I should have and didn't want to keep you waiting any further," I said.

Her harsh expression softened.

"Sweet girl. You are so thoughtful. Next time, finish your breakfast and then come find me."

"Yes, Mama."

Maeve waved Catherine away, keeping her contemplative gaze on me.

"You look refreshed today," she commented.

"A benefit from the extra sleep I believe," I said. A part of me wondered if she would prevent me from sleeping so much in the future.

"Finish your biscuit, and then begin reading again," she said, pointing at the book that waited near the chair I'd used the day before.

"Yes, Mama."

Reading the stories a second time proved more entertaining. I lost myself to those worlds and let my imagination free instead of trying to analyze the stories for clues. By the time Catherine announced lunch, I was already halfway through them.

"Have you learned why your sister wanted you to read the book?" Maeve asked as the four of us sat at the table.

"I haven't yet, but perhaps I will before I reach the end again," I said, carefully choosing my words.

"Tell me about the stories," Maeve said.

"The first is about a boy who won't share his bread with a beggar. The beggar is secretly a caster who turns him into a toad for his greed then makes him into a soup and eats him."

Maeve's smile became genuine. Or as genuine as I'd yet to see.

"That tale sounds entertaining. And the next?"

"The next is about another boy, separate from the first and in another town. He steals a pie from the window of an old woman. Like the first story, she too possesses knowledge of magic and curses the boy, removing his ability to taste any food or drink. He dies slowly, starving himself because nothing pleases him."

Maeve considered me thoughtfully.

"I may need to read these tales. They sound lovely."

"I do like them," I said.

"Does the next one also mention someone who does magic?"

"Not someone but something. An enchanted well that grants wishes, but they all go horribly wrong."

She sighed.

"For the remainder of the day, I think it would be best if you work on straightening your room. You're not sleeping as well as you should where you are. And, sleeping before the hearth is not befitting for one of my daughters."

"Yes, Mama," I said. I glanced at Porcia, who met my gaze. Were we wondering the same thing? Would I be sharing my old room with her?

When we finished our meal, Maeve asked me to follow her. She led me to the attic door and unlocked it with a key. It had never been locked before.

We ascended the stairs, and I noted how Father's things had been shoved into the free space, once again cluttering what Kellen had tried to organize.

"It will take some time, but I'm sure you'll set this mess to rights," Maeve said.

I glanced at her, unsure of her meaning.

"Mama?"

"This is your room, my sweet. The largest in the house for the child I hold very dear. I'll call you for supper," she said before leaving me.

I listened to the door close and the lock slide into place. Turning, I looked around my new prison and felt a sense of relief. Locked in the attic wouldn't be so horrible. It was colder up here, but I also knew there were several comfortable beds, extra blankets, and even some of Mother's old clothes. I wouldn't freeze. At least, not until winter.

Before that gloomy thought could take hold, I set to work. I chose a spot in one corner of the attic near the chimney that came from Mother's old room. The heat from it would help warm my space, and I also had a small window for light.

Around my chosen area, I moved the bigger pieces of furniture into place, which took time and effort. On top of them, I began stacking smaller furniture I knew I wouldn't use. Eventually, I created two walls that reached the rafters. Using the oilcloths, I covered them both and looked around my cozy space. It was large enough for two beds, should Kellen be found.

Leaving my bedroom area, I surveyed the rest of the attic. So much furniture remained that I hadn't needed to touch the little cubby that Kellen discovered, or use Mother's or Father's furniture. I pulled the soft chair from Mother's room into a bit of clear space and sat for a few moments, tired and in pain.

As the light began to fade, I started to wonder if I would have the strength to set up my bed for the night.

A key turned in the lock below and the door opened.

"Miss?" Catherine called. "I brought you candles and a lamp."

Her footfalls echoed on the stairs as I struggled to rise from the chair. I saw her reach the top and look at the large, covered stack of furniture that made up one wall of my new room.

"What do you think?" I asked, coming to stand beside her.

"I think you've pushed yourself too far," she said. She looked me over. "You'll need a longer soak in the salt water bath tonight before you sleep."

I gave her a wry smile and followed her into the area I'd made.

"It likely won't do me any good. I've yet to set up my bed."

She put the candles and the lamp down.

"I'll do that. Just show me where the bed is."

She and I worked together to set up the two twin beds. She didn't comment on my insistence for a second one, and I didn't explain myself. It wasn't that I thought Kellen would be captured. I only wanted it to appear that I thought that way. It would likely appease Maeve. And I wanted to appease her. I wanted her to let her guard down. Not that I intended to run—I wasn't yet well enough to go farther than the drive or to willingly leave Catherine and Heather to their own fates. No, I wanted Maeve to believe I was falling in line with her plans so she would share them with me.

Catherine and I made up both beds with the blankets that we found in one of the trunks. They smelled a bit musty, but I didn't mind. I knew they would air out in the drafty attic space. We added a table and brought the chair inside the space as well. It was comfortably cozy, yet still had more space than my previous room.

"Nicely done," Maeve said from the opening to my space, startling both Catherine and me.

I looked up and watched her study the walls.

"You're more clever than you credit yourself." Maeve met my gaze. "It's time for dinner."

"Yes, Mama," I said, moving to join her. I didn't look at Catherine or thank her, feeling that it would be unwise to call attention to her.

I followed Maeve downstairs, wincing at each step. My legs hurt fiercely from climbing up on things. My arms and ribs hurt more from all of the lifting. I most certainly would benefit from a bath after dinner.

Joining Cecilia and Porcia, who already waited at the table, we ate a quiet meal. I stifled more yawns than I could count and could feel Maeve's gaze on me. She didn't comment, though.

When she finished, she sat back in her chair and studied me.

"Your concern for your sister hasn't escaped my notice," she said.

I kept my expression carefully blank.

"I want her home as badly as you do. Each time I check the mirror for her, however, I cannot tell where she is. I thought the book might help us, but perhaps you know the place." She leaned forward in her chair. "You will tell me if the place looks familiar, won't you?"

"Yes, Mama."

Her eyes narrowed ever so slightly, and I wondered what answer she'd wanted if not that one.

"The trees didn't look familiar to me. But all I know are the woods here and town," I said, repeating Hugh's assessment of my knowledge.

"I think, perhaps, it's time we look again."

Porcia and Cecilia rose with her. I hurried to do the same, wincing at the ache in my legs from sitting so long.

The mirror remained in the foyer, uncovered and now mounted to the wall.

Maeve stood before it, gave it a kiss, then repeated the words from the day before.

"Mirror, Mirror against the wall, I summon you now to answer my call. Show me Kellen."

The glass shimmered with magic again, and once the green faded along with our reflections, Kellen appeared. Her mourning dress was ripped in places, and she had scratches on her skin. However, the state of her dress concerned me less than the fact that she was fast asleep, which I found odd given the time of day. I studied the image, noting her long braid trailed out behind her, ending somewhere off the edge and that the blanket under her looked coarsely woven. Rough and slightly frayed.

"I don't recognize anything," I said, just as I caught the edge of her braid move ever so slightly. So focused on my sister and the relief she was safe and resting, I didn't recognize I was opening my mouth to speak until my words emerged without thought.

"I think someone is with her. Her braid just moved." I wanted to take my words back as soon as I said them.

Maeve stopped studying me and studied the mirror. The braid moved again. Her black hair in the dim lighting against the dark blanket made it hard to see, but it was there nonetheless.

Silently, I cursed the spell compelling me to speak the truth to Maeve.

"Show me who is with Kellen," Maeve commanded. The mirror went dark.

I frowned, and Cecilia and Porcia gasped.

"Surely, she's not—"

Maeve lifted her hand, silencing Porcia.

"I doubt she's with Prince Greydon. Likely she found herself a caster, thinking another will be able to help her." Based on the humor lacing Maeve's words, I knew Maeve believed the opposite.

She looked at me again.

"Does anything else catch your eye, Eloise?"

I studied my sister's peaceful face for a moment longer, memorizing her features as if this would be my last chance to see her.

"I'm sorry, Mama. Nothing is recognizable or familiar to me except my sister."

Maeve didn't get angry this time. She only nodded and asked to see the tracker. The man now sat near a fire. He looked older, and his eyes moved relentlessly as he watched the dark. Wherever he was, he gave the impression he wasn't safe.

"Do you recognize this place?" Maeve asked.

I shook my head slowly, gaze affixed to the mirror. Behind the man, something flickered. I stepped closer, involuntarily drawn. I barely noticed Maeve step away as I focused on the space beyond the man's shoulders.

The flicker came again as the flames before the image of the man flared then diminished.

"Eyes," I said softly, fighting to tamp down my joy.

The tracker might be hunting my sister, but something was hunting him as well.

CHAPTER SIX

I LAY IN MY BED, READING THE BOOK FROM MY SISTER BY THE light of a candle. The bath Maeve had allowed me, after I had pointed out that her hunter was being hunted, hadn't been a salt bath, but a hot bath filled with pungent herbs.

She'd washed my hair and spoke to me kindly as she worked. Every touch had been gentle and caring. That was my reward for being helpful. While I was grateful not to ache as I lay down to sleep, I wasn't foolish enough to want to continue to help Maeve, no matter what anguish it might save me.

I thought of my sister, laying so peacefully, and my heart ached. I missed her with every breath and hoped she was safe from whatever hunted the tracker. Yawning, I tried to focus on the next story but failed. Instead of wasting more of the candle, I blew it out and snuggled under the covers.

It felt as if I'd no sooner closed my eyes than I opened them again. However, the light coming through the window told me I'd slept a full night. I used the chamber pot then the washbasin Catherine had set up for me.

I'd only just laced up my dress when I heard the key turn in my door.

"Eloise, it's time for breakfast. Please bring the book."

I grabbed the book and moved quickly to the stairs.

"Did you sleep well?" Maeve asked as I descended.

"Yes, Mama. Thank you for the bath. It was lovely."

She smiled at me, her expression conveying a fondness for me that I doubted she had ever felt.

"I'm relieved to hear it helped. Is your room comfortable?" she asked, closing the door and leading the way to the stairs.

"Very. Thank you for considering our need for more space," I said. "Kellen will be pleased when she's home again."

Maeve turned sharply, studying me. Whatever she saw on my face seemed to content her because she continued to the dining room without further comment.

"I believe we've spent enough idle time here," Maeve said. "The visitors have stopped appearing of their own volition. Like us, I believe they tire of waiting to hear word of the prince's arrival. It's time to adapt."

Catherine and Heather entered the room and served our breakfast of hot oats. Maeve waited until they left again to continue.

"Cecilia, I believe you'll have more opportunity closer to the castle." Maeve reached into her pocket and withdrew a vial. "Porcia, I'd like you to go to the market." She handed each girl a vial.

"Where will you be, Mama?" Cecilia asked.

"I will start with the Houses. Many will have heard my name by now, thanks to my loyal followers."

The girls smiled and started eating their oats.

"What about me, Mama?" I asked.

Maeve paused with a spoon halfway to her mouth.

"How can I help?" I added.

She set her spoon down and clasped my hand across the table.

"Sweet child, you will have your chance to help soon."

I suppressed the shiver of dread that wanted to run through me at her words.

She released me and returned to her meal. I slowly did the same, the food curdling in my stomach. Before the tracker located my sister, I needed to know what Maeve planned for Kellen and me. Why had Maeve spared us, and what was she doing here? Yet, pressing for information would not help me. It would only make Maeve suspicious. I would continue to recover and read the book to discover where Kellen might be so I could join her when the time was right.

I STOOD at the attic window, looking out at the trees and blue sky. It was a beautiful day, and more than anything, I wished I could walk out in the sun.

It had been more than a week since Kellen left and four days since I moved into the attic. Yet, there was no sign of help, which made me worry more for Kellen.

Sighing, I glanced at my chair where the book waited. Each day Maeve and her daughters went to town only to return each evening in a more foul mood. Maeve hadn't even asked me about the book last night, which both relieved and worried me. While Maeve's distraction meant I could focus on trying to discover why Kellen wanted me to read the book, I couldn't help but feel a sense of foreboding at what might have a greater priority to Maeve than finding Kellen.

Restless, I paced the path I'd created in the attic and focused on what I'd read. The only common theme within the stories was magic. In some way, each character was touched by it. But, I didn't understand where the message might be in that. Kellen and I had been touched by magic the moment the necklace arrived. The book was a bit late to serve as a warning for that. It either had to be a clue to where she went or a clue to something else she'd discovered.

I returned to my chair, determined to try again, and opened the book at random. The page was in the middle of the story of the enchanted well. One old woman had grown smart and started choosing her words with more care so that the well would grant her precisely what she wanted. I felt much like the old woman. Every time Maeve asked a question, the compulsion to answer honestly almost had me blurting my thoughts without the respectful wording or tone that Maeve expected. Also, like the old woman, I learned there are half-truths that could satisfy the spell.

However, I didn't think that was the warning Kellen meant. I shifted in my seat. While my bruising had mostly faded, and I breathed with ease once again, the chair wasn't comfortable. There was something in the back padding that continually dug into my spine. Frustrated, I twisted in my seat, prepared to poke at the backing when the book fell to the floor. I cringed and hoped I hadn't damaged the spine. Mr. Bentwell would never let me—

I swallowed hard as I remembered Mr. Bentwell's fate and that he would never see the book again.

Leaning to pick up the volume, I saw the spine had indeed pulled away from the pages. Tears of frustration mixed with sorrow gathered in my eyes. I hated that I was locked up here and that Kellen was out there. Somewhere. Mostly, I hated not doing anything.

As I picked up the book, a small slip of paper fell to the floor. Heart fluttering, I picked it up and read it.

This is but one book of many. Read them all for me. ~K

I stared at the note, dumbfounded. That was it? She wanted me to read more? I thought of poor Mr. Bentwell and wondered what, exactly, Kellen would have wanted me to read there. Her romance books? I scoffed at the idea even as my gaze swung to the back corner of the attic.

There was only one set of books that had interested Kellen after Maeve's arrival. The books of magic. Since being locked up, I'd been too nervous to venture into the hidden space that Kellen had found. Maeve tended to want me downstairs at the most unexpected times.

I chewed my lip and checked the window. No one was home now.

Decided, I quietly crossed the space and climbed into the small burrow. The books weren't where I last saw them. Instead of stacked neatly in the open, I found them wrapped and tucked away in Mother's trunk.

On a whim, I checked for the King's letter and found it missing. In its place, I found another note.

My throat tightened as I recognized my sister's neat writing.

IF YOU FIND THIS, I'm likely gone. You were chained and beaten for our attempt to leave. Maeve locked me up here to store away Father's things. I took some time to read. Read what you can. There's knowledge in words. Perhaps you will find an answer where I did not. There must be a connection between our home and what's happened to us. I took the letter for safe keeping as I believe it's what Maeve was searching for as we went through Father's things. I'll find him and bring him home. He's the only one who can help us now.

. . .

DREAD FILLED my heart as I understood where my sister had gone and why I'd glimpsed her running in terror. The tracker's fear now made more sense, too. Tales of the Dark Forest were told to children the moment they were born. No one entered the dark woods if they wanted to live. No one except my foolish, brave sister.

I folded the letter and tucked it back into place, tears blurring my vision. Without looking at the books or the letters from Elspeth, I left the burrow and returned to my chair.

The sun slowly sank as I sat there trying to sort through what I knew. Outside, the sound of hooves brought me out of my own thoughts. I rose and caught a glimpse of the rider before he rounded the house.

The tracker had returned, and he'd been alone. I paced back and forth, worrying my lip. Surely Maeve hadn't ordered for Kellen to be killed. Maeve had said Kellen and I were important to her and asked that Kellen be returned alive first, her safety a condition on my behavior. And I had behaved. I'd done everything Maeve had asked of me. My gaze fell on the book. Everything except for determining where my sister had gone. Was that why Maeve had stopped asking about the book? Because Kellen was dead?

Fear twisted my middle until I was sick with it, and no amount of pacing alleviated my anguish as I watched the window for my tormentor's return.

It took another hour before the carriage rolled into the yard. I hurried to the stairway, a bundle of nervous energy. The lock turned in the door almost immediately.

"Your mother would like you to join them in the sitting room," Catherine said when she saw me already descending.

"Any news?" I asked softly.

"The man didn't speak to us."

I hastened to the sitting room and found Maeve, Cecilia, and Porcia already comfortably seated. The tracker stood before them, a displeased scowl on his face. New lines marked the skin around his eyes and strands of white now intermingled with his dark hair.

"Here, Eloise," Maeve said, patting the chair to her left.

I quickly sat, watching Maeve.

"Thank you for waiting," she said to the man. "Tell us what you've learned and why you've returned without my daughter." Her words to the tracker and the underlying note of threat in them relieved me.

"She's in the Dark Forest," he said bluntly. He withdrew the box from his jacket pocket and handed it to Maeve. "The box led me straight to her, but something was hunting her. When it caught my scent, it started hunting me, too. The fire kept it at bay at night. Using that box kept it away during the day. It didn't like the magic."

"The girl," Maeve said lowly. "Where is she?"

"She found a cottage before I could get to her. There's a

group of little men there guarding it. I couldn't get past them."

"Little men?" Maeve asked.

The man held out his hand at thigh height and raising it to about his waist.

"Somewhere in that range," he said.

"You couldn't defeat a group of short men?"

"Short, My Lady. Not weak."

From the corner of my eye, I watched Maeve's expression change from slightly annoyed to pleasant and charming.

"Is there anything else helpful you can tell us?"

"The cottage is in a sunny clearing."

"How is that helpful?" she asked.

"Your girl is stuck there until someone saves her. She'll never make it past the beast a second time, now that it knows she's there."

"Hmm," Maeve said, tapping her chin lightly. "I suppose that is helpful to know." She looked at me. "Are you content with the information he's provided?"

I looked at the tracker.

"Can you tell me more about these little men? Why were they defending her?"

"They weren't. They were defending their home. Not sure they even knew she was inside. With them at my front and the beast at my back, I didn't have much choice but to leave and return with this news while I could still tell it."

I looked at Maeve, trying to gauge if I'd heard

everything or if something had been said before I'd arrived. What proof did I have that my sister was still alive?

"How do we know his words are true?" I asked.

Maeve smiled at me and lifted a hand to stroke my cheek at the area that still held a hint of fading bruise.

"You are a smart one, Eloise. Never doubt that."

She went to the man. Before I knew what was happening, blood showered my skirt, the carpet, and Maeve as the man clutched at his throat. The glint of light near Maeve's hand drew my eye to the blade she still held before I looked back at the tracker. I blinked at the red cascading through the man's fingers as he gasped and choked. Only Maeve's firm grip on his shoulder kept him standing.

"Let honest words spill from your lips as quickly as the blood spills from your throat. Does Kellen still live?"

"Yes," the man rasped.

"Can she escape the wood on her own?" she asked.

"No."

He gurgled and fell to the carpet, jerking as what remained of his vitality was inhaled by Maeve.

She gave a satisfied sigh and looked at Porcia.

"Please fetch Hugh."

Porcia left the room at a calm pace as if her pretty yellow skirt wasn't dotted with blood.

"Cecilia, can you let Heather and Catherine know we'll need to wash before dinner. Also, let them know they'll need to tidy in here as soon as possible."

Cecilia nodded and went to do as Maeve asked.

Stunned, I sat in my chair and stared at the dead man. Maeve noticed and returned to the chair beside me.

"Are you all right, my sweet?" she asked.

"Yes, Mama," I said though I was far from okay. While the death was gruesome and terrifying, that alone hadn't sent my heart racing. Kellen was still in the Dark Forest, protected only by a patch of sunlight and little men.

"Perhaps I'm not all right," I said.

"Tell me what troubles you."

"Kellen was alive when he last saw her, but how do we know she still is?"

Maeve patted my hand.

"You love your sister so. Let us check."

Maeve took my hand and led me from the room. I listened to her call upon her mirror and waited for the image of my sister. Once again, it showed her sleeping. It wasn't like her to sleep so early in the day. And it was most unlike her to sleep on the dirt.

I stared at her peaceful face, unsure what to do next. If what the tracker said was true, Kellen could no longer help me. Instead, she needed my help. But, how could I help her without endangering her further?

"What are you thinking?" Maeve asked.

"It's not like her to sleep so early," I said, choosing the safest thought to share. "Who has Kellen? Why can't we see them?"

Maeve tried again to get the mirror to show her the

home where Kellen slept at night or the people who protected her. But, the first question only showed our home and the second showed me.

Maeve turned to me, an angry light in her eyes.

"Go to the dining room and wait for me there. This mirror vexes me."

I hurriedly left, and listened to the echo of the wooden rod smack against the mirror behind me.

In the dining room, I calmly took my seat at the table and checked my clothing. I'd never been so grateful to wear black. No visual reminder of the scene I just witnessed remained.

After the noise in the hall quieted, Maeve joined me, followed by Cecilia then Porcia. Catherine and Heather began serving a meal of roasted quail in brandied briarberry sauce on a bed of new spring greens. Catherine glanced at me as she set the plate before Porcia but quickly looked away. Did Heather and she think I was now under Maeve's thumb? Would they wonder if I had a part in what happened in the sitting room?

I daintily cut into the quail Heather had set before me and took my first bite.

"This is lovely," I said to no one in particular, keeping my focus on my food.

"You're quite right," Maeve said. "Thank you for preparing such a delicious meal, Heather and Catherine. Your hard work for this family is noticed and very appreciated."

"Thank you, My Lady," they both said quietly.

As they left the room, I hoped my praise had answered the question of whether or not I was involved.

"Girls, it would seem our first tracker failed us. I cannot, in good conscience, leave Kellen in danger in the Dark Forest. Tomorrow we must locate good, able-bodied men who will not run in fear at the sight of a beastie in the trees."

"Yes, Mama," both Cecilia and Porcia said between bites.

I could barely focus on my food as my mind raced. For certain, more than one question had been answered this evening. I now knew how Mr. Bentwell had died, and I also knew that Kellen wasn't yet out of danger from Maeve.

After dinner, I returned to my room where I once again read the book of fairy tales by the lamp's light. This time out of boredom rather than necessity. A whisper of noise pulled me from the story. I listened closely and heard it again.

Picking up the lamp, I left the bed and walked lightly across the floor. I followed the sound to the outside wall near the stairs. It seemed a voice was coming from under a stack of chairs. Moving them quietly, I found a vent in the floor.

Words drifted up to me, and I leaned closer to hear.

"...ruined my favorite dress," Cecilia said. "Blood never truly comes out. Now I have to draw from my store of power to remove it by other means. These are costly mistakes."

"Perhaps the mistake is using your power to clean a dress. It's better to purchase a new one," Porcia said.

Cecilia snorted.

"If we knew there was time, perhaps. But we don't know when he'll arrive, do we?"

Porcia sighed.

"No. We don't. I can't believe not a single person of worth knows where the prince is. He left before we did. He should be here by now. If we were in town, we would probably learn more."

Something creaked.

"Mama," Porcia said. "I didn't mean—"

"Quiet. You did mean. Cecilia, stop wasting your magic on cleaning silly gowns. Porcia is right in that. She's also right about no one of worth knowing anything. We've been overlooking the obvious. It's not someone of worth who would know the prince's whereabouts." A slap sounded in the room. "Even if we lived in town, we would know nothing more than we do now. This home is the gateway to the castle. Tomorrow, after we return from town, I will remove your doubt."

CHAPTER SEVEN

PORCIA HAD BEEN EXCEPTIONALLY QUIET AT BREAKFAST, AND I couldn't help but wonder if she was fearing how her mother planned to remove her doubt once they returned from town. Most likely.

My stepsister's fear probably equaled my own, though for different reasons. Why were they trying to learn when the prince would arrive? How did they believe our home was a gateway to the castle? Because of proximity? I was tempted to tell Maeve that I'd never once seen any of the Royal family, despite living on the King's lands.

A lock slid in the door, and Catherine called out for me.

"I've brought your tray, miss."

I hurried to the top of the stairs and watched her ascend. Behind her, the door closed and locked as it had every day Maeve was gone and the midday meal could not be served in the dining room.

"I'm sorry you have to carry it up here," I said.

"There's no need to apologize." She met my gaze as she reached the top. "Heather and I know this is not your doing."

The way she said the words while holding my gaze brought tears of relief to my eyes. I quickly turned away and nodded, hating that I could not speak openly to her. Hating that she would be forced to repeat our conversation to Maeve, compelled by the same spell that bound me.

"I've brought you a nice stew and fresh biscuits," she said, moving around me to set the tray on a small table beside a chair I'd placed outside of my room. The chair was one from the pile I'd moved in order to better hear the conversation in Cecilia's room. I'd spent some time this morning uncovering all the vents under the guise of creating a sitting area for myself.

"It looks nice up here," Catherine said hesitantly as I took a seat.

"It's more spacious than I need," I said. "But it suits me well."

She lifted the lid from the soup bowl and uncovered the biscuits.

"Is there anything else you need before I take the chamber pot?" she asked.

I shook my head.

"Thank you, Catherine, to you and Heather both, for taking such good care of me."

"As your mother requested," Catherine said.

"Yes, as Mama requested."

She nodded, gave my shoulder a light squeeze, and went to my room for the chamber pot. I started to eat, my thoughts wandering back to what Maeve and her daughters were doing in town. I hoped they wouldn't find more trackers. Although the Dark Forest was dangerous, Kellen was safely out of Maeve's reach. That meant I could run when the time was right. But only if I could get Catherine and Heather to run with me.

"Have you given any thought where you would like to travel, if you could travel anywhere?" I asked.

Catherine gave me a knowing look.

"There's nowhere else I would rather be than here, miss. This place calls to me like no other. Don't let my lack of dreams influence yours," she said.

I wasn't certain, but it sounded like she was trying to tell me to run. While I watched, she began to roll back the sleeve of her gown. On the inside of her elbow, I saw a red mark that resembled the faint outline of a raven.

It was too perfect to be a birthmark, which could only mean that Maeve had done something to her.

"I think it's healthy for all young girls to dream a bit. Just so you keep your head where it's supposed to be."

And where, I wondered, was that? Unable to ask directly, I focused instead on her mark. "This soup is delicious. Leeks?"

Catherine nodded.

"Who goes to town for supplies?" I asked.

"Hugh," she said. "Heather and I provide a list of what we need so we can stay where we belong."

With that, I understood. Maeve had magically bound Heather and Catherine to the estate. Even if they wanted to run, they wouldn't be able to. And if I ran, they would suffer.

I set my spoon down and looked out the small window.

"The soup displeases you, miss?" Catherine asked quietly, and I knew we weren't speaking of the soup but her answer.

"Confined to this attic on a sunny day displeases me," I said bluntly. "I miss the sun and the wind and the sound of the trees. I miss visiting my mother's grave. I miss my sister."

She nodded, a sorrowful expression on her face, then left with the chamber pot.

I managed to finish the soup after it had long gone cold and clouds began to blot out the sun. I'd only just put the spoon aside again when I heard the rattle of an approaching carriage. I rose and checked the window.

Maeve had returned, but not alone. Several riders followed.

I hurriedly moved to the attic door to wait. Heather opened it several minutes later.

"Your mother is waiting for you in the sitting room."

I was already passing Heather and racing down the stairs. At the last moment, I slowed and entered the sitting room at a serene pace. Maeve stood in the center of the room with Cecilia and Porcia on each side of her but a step back. Before Maeve, with their backs to the windows, stood a group of five men. They all watched me enter.

"Good afternoon, Mama," I said, only looking at Maeve.

Maeve smiled and gestured to a chair against a wall. The simple unspoken command was clear. I was here to observe but not interfere.

I sat and watched Maeve face the men. She held her hand out to Cecilia, who placed five gold coins in her palm.

"By accepting a coin, you are binding yourself to my service," Maeve said. "Do you understand?"

The men nodded, and she handed each of them a coin. The moment they took them, a green light flashed in their eyes. I wondered if they were even aware they were now under her spell. I recalled Timmy Bell, and his reaction, and guessed that they did not.

"My daughter, Kellen, is missing," Maeve said. "She's in a cottage in the Dark Forest. I need you to go to her and await my command."

One of the men looked down at the coin.

"A gold piece to risk our lives in the Dark Forest? We all know the tales. There are creatures in those trees that will turn a man into a beast with a bite."

"If they don't eat you first," another man said.

"The gold coin is not payment but protection. So long as you have it on your person, no beast made of magic will be able to harm you."

"How do we know it will work?" the first man asked.

Cecilia picked up a lamp and began softly chanting words I couldn't quite hear. As I watched, the lamp blurred its appearance, changing like the mirror when it shifted images. It melted into the form of a small dog.

"Bite the man," Cecilia said.

The dog darted forward and jumped up to clamp down on the man's hand. The man lifted his arm and looked at the dog dangling from his fingers.

"Are you hurt?" Maeve asked.

"Not a bit," the man answered.

"Are you done questioning my authority and knowledge, or do you need further proof of the magic of which I'm capable?"

I saw the exact moment they all realized the precariousness of their situation.

"We need no proof, My Lady," the stockiest man said with a slight bow. "We are in your service and follow your command."

She smiled at the man.

"What is your name?"

"Grimm."

"A fine name," she said with a smile. "I believe fate led you to me, Grimm. You shall lead these men and report to me once you find my daughter. Kellen is a rare beauty, like her sister, with ebony hair and bright blue eyes. She's intelligent. Do not disregard her because of her gender."

She handed Grimm the box.

"To find her, have one of your men use this box." As

with the previous tracker, she explained how the box worked, the cost of using it, and the purpose of the ribbon. Then Maeve held out her hand to Porcia. Her daughter handed over a blade, and I braced myself.

There was no throat slashing this time, though. Maeve took the man's hand and pricked his finger. His gaze never left her as she lifted it to her lips. A soft grunt escaped him the moment her mouth closed over the tip, and the front of his pants stirred as she began to suckle his finger. My cheeks heated as he moaned and closed his eyes.

When she released him, he looked at her, his eyes blazing green.

"We are bound now, Grimm," she said. "You can speak to me whenever you wish through any reflective surface. All you need to do is call my name. Maeve."

"I belong to you and only you," he said, the words reminiscent of Hugh's.

"I know," she said, releasing him. "And when you successfully complete your task and return to me, I will reward you in ways you cannot possibly imagine."

The man's gaze heated.

"Go," she said gently. "Fulfill my will. Find my daughter, and report to me. Do not return until I ask it of you."

He nodded, and the group left the room.

"Cecilia. Porcia. Please let Heather and Catherine know we're expecting guests tonight. Then go prepare yourselves. We'll take what little remains."

After they too left, Maeve crossed the room and sat

beside me. She took my hand, her fingers squeezing me gently.

"Have no doubt they will find and retrieve your sister. I will not fail to reunite you again."

"Thank you, Mama."

"You asked what you could do to help, and I do have a task for you. Do you recall the prince's servant? The one you thought killed your mother?"

It took everything I had not to jerk from her touch at the mention of Kaven. It felt like a lifetime ago since I'd last laid eyes on the man that I'd mistakenly suspected of wrongdoing. So much had changed since then that I'd all but forgotten him.

"Yes," I said.

She tilted her head at me.

"Yes, Mama."

She smiled.

"I would like you to get to know him. I need you to gain his trust and confidence. Can you do that?"

My heart raced with excitement as my mind raced with the possibilities this opportunity might present. In order for me to gain Kaven's confidence, Maeve would need to let me out of the attic. I would be able to run. I briefly thought of Catherine and Heather then of Kellen. If I ran before the trackers reached her maybe—

"Do you think I ask too much?" Maeve asked.

I immediately regretted my silence.

"I'm not sure," I said honestly. "I wasn't very nice to him

in the past. I'm afraid he might not be willing to spend time with me."

Maeve smiled widely.

"He's a man. I promise he will want to spend time with you if you approach him correctly."

Catherine entered the room.

"I beg your pardon, My Lady. How many guests should we prepare for tonight?"

"There will be twenty. Just a light meal. No need to waste good food on them. You can serve us a full meal afterward."

Confusion clouded Catherine's gaze, but she nodded and left the room. I was less confused. Whatever Maeve planned tonight, I doubted the men who arrived would see another sunrise after they entered our doors.

I STOOD before Maeve in the entry. Dressed in my finest mourning gown with my hair piled high, I endured her appraising gaze.

"You are quite lovely, Eloise," she said. "Dare I say...you might even be lovelier than my own daughters."

"Thank you, Mama," I said.

She made a non-committal noise.

"Catherine mentioned that you miss your walks outside. Why didn't you tell me?"

"I didn't want to appear ungrateful," I said. It was a very

true statement. I feared what Maeve would do if I showed her anything but gratitude. Yet, saying what I had in front of Catherine had been a purposeful thing. I wanted Maeve to know I was chafing for a bit of freedom but not acting on those urges. I'd hoped it would help further win Maeve's trust.

"You should always speak freely with me," she said. "I want to know what you're thinking at all times."

Her amulet pulsed with life as she spoke the words. The familiar warmth wrapped around me. I raged against it, mentally pushing it away. I wouldn't tell her everything. What secrets I had were mine to keep. And, for the safety of Kellen, I could not tell Maeve everything. The warmth drifted away instead of seeping into my bones.

"Go on," Maeve said. "Tell me."

Nothing compelled me to speak. Shock rippled through me, and I masked it quickly with rash words.

"I want you to stop casting spells on me and treat me like a real daughter."

Maeve's eyes widened then she hugged me hard.

"My precious girl," she said against my ear. "I am treating you like my own daughter. Never doubt that."

I hugged her tightly in return and pitied Cecilia and Porcia if Maeve spoke the truth. When she released me, she stood by my side, holding my hand. Together, we waited to greet the first round of Maeve's victims.

"I hope Catherine and Heather make something sweet

to follow dinner," I said randomly, knowing she would expect such things if the spell had worked.

Maeve's fingers twitched in mine, and she chuckled.

"You will make me proud, Eloise," Maeve said. "Of that, I am certain."

I doubted that very much. I'd seen the way she'd beaten the mirror in anger and knew pride wasn't what she would feel when I finally ran. I almost wished I could be there to see it.

The first carriage approached, distracting me from my pleasant thoughts. Maeve released me to greet the men and direct them to the dining room. When all twenty had arrived, we joined them.

Catherine and Heather immediately began to serve a cold soup, enduring a few grabs and fondles from the men as they did so.

"Thank you all for joining us tonight," Maeve said. "Especially on such short notice. I hope you've continued your discretion about our meetings."

A glimmer of green light flashed in the eyes of all but one man.

"William, who have you told?" Maeve asked.

"My son, My Lady. I wanted him to join us tonight. I said nothing of what happens here, only that I was attending and wanted him to accompany me."

"You could not persuade him?" she asked.

"No. His wife just gave birth to their first babe. He chose to return home to her."

"You should have told him he'd get his cock sucked," one of the men said with a chuckle. "It would have convinced him."

Maeve smiled.

"I'm sure it would have. It's a pity he couldn't be here."

During the conversation, Catherine and Heather finished serving the men and took our bowls away.

"Why aren't you eating?" William asked, spoon partway to his mouth.

"We're waiting for the next course," Maeve said. "It's important not to overindulge and to preserve our figures. Don't you agree, Porcia?"

"Yes, Mama."

The men grunted their agreement and ate their soups. I studied Porcia's downturned gaze, realizing there was reproach in Maeve's words.

"Heather. Catherine," Maeve called abruptly before anyone finished their soup.

Already bare, the women entered the dining room.

"Show these men how a woman is meant to be loved," Maeve said.

My mouth dropped open in shock as Catherine turned to Heather and started kissing her. The men watched raptly, encouraging them to tweak each other's nipples and "slip a finger into her twattle." I turned away from what Heather and Catherine were doing and watched Maeve and her daughters.

As Heather and Catherine kissed passionately, the

three women stood, each with a knife clutched in her hand. Maeve's amulet glowed brightly, and the men's eyes flashed bright green in response. They quieted but continued to watch the maids.

"Cecilia, you may have three," Maeve said. "Porcia, one should suffice. The rest are mine."

Cecilia and Porcia each positioned themselves behind a man as did Maeve. While I couldn't see what her daughters did, I could clearly watch Maeve.

With the knife, she pricked the back of the man's neck. He made a small sound, just enough to part his lips and allow the green light to escape. None of the men turned to look. The sounds that Heather and Catherine were making might have covered his gasp, but certainly the light was noticeable as it fed Maeve's amulet.

Twin lights came from the men Cecilia and Porcia had chosen, then disappeared into the chests of their gowns.

But, it was Maeve who had my attention. She went from man to man, doing the same to each until sixteen strands of green flowed toward her breast. The first man's features hollowed, echoing the look that I'd briefly glimpsed on Hugh. He thumped limply against the table, his gaze never leaving Catherine and Heather.

Maeve waved her hand, cutting off the thread. One by one she fed from them. Her skin began to glow with the power she gained.

"Return to your homes and make love to your wives.

Remember nothing but the pleasure you received here," Maeve said.

Catherine and Heather broke apart as soon as the men stood and left the room.

"We're ready for our meal, now," Maeve said, returning to her seat.

I desperately wanted to offer to serve the meal in Catherine's and Heather's places but knew Maeve wouldn't approve. So I held my tongue and stared at the table.

"What are your thoughts, Eloise? You're very quiet."

I looked up to find Maeve studying me intently.

"I didn't realize you had used so much power on the trackers."

"I didn't. This harvest was for what I plan to do next."

The door opened, and Catherine and Heather entered with our covered plates.

"Perfect timing," Maeve said. "I'm famished."

CHAPTER EIGHT

I'D BARELY EATEN HALF MY HOT OATS WHEN A THUNDEROUS knocking at the main entry disturbed the silence. Surprised, I looked at Maeve. How hadn't we heard anything?

"Would you like me to answer the door, Mama?" Porcia asked, setting her spoon aside.

"Not this time. Heather," Maeve called.

Heather rushed from the kitchen.

"Yes, My Lady."

"Please answer the door."

Heather nodded and hurried to the main entry.

"Eat," Maeve said softly.

I brought my spoon to my mouth as I strained to hear Heather's softly spoken greeting. Approaching footfalls echoed against the floor. I glanced at Maeve, who calmly took a bite of her oats.

A moment later, a King's Guard entered the dining room ahead of Heather. The guard was finally here. After all this time. And to what good? I briefly considered what would happen if I attempted to tell the man anything of significance. I would choke on my words, for certain, and once they left, Kellen or I would certainly suffer for the attempt. I held my tongue and waited.

"Good morning, ladies," the guard said with a slight bow. "By the King's order, I have been asked to search your dwelling."

He withdrew a rolled piece of parchment from his jacket and offered it to Maeve as Heather scurried back to the kitchen. Her gaze briefly met mine, and I wondered if she'd thought the same thing about speaking.

Maeve glanced at the parchment then at the man as she set her spoon aside and wiped her mouth with her napkin.

"Your uniform and word are enough proof for me, Captain. Of course you may search as you've been ordered. Perhaps I can assist you in locating whatever it is you need."

"Your assistance is not required. Please remain seated and finish your morning meal. My sergeant-at-arms will remain with you in the event you have any questions while we complete the search."

He nodded to us as another man stepped into the room, then the captain left. The sergeant-at-arms' stoic expression didn't suggest he remained with us to answer questions but rather to contain us within the dining room.

I considered him for a long moment, trying desperately to think of a way to alert him of Maeve's actions. However, even that thought created a slight constriction in my throat.

"Eat, girls. I'm sure this is nothing more than a search for some errant servant who stole away with a crown jewel," Maeve said dismissively before taking a bite.

I struggled to do the same and not choke. Since I couldn't alert the guards, I decided to hope they would find something incriminating instead. However, if they did, I knew I might also be prosecuted since I was now officially Maeve's daughter as well. But I was willing to take the risk in order to free Catherine and Heather. Perhaps, if I was allowed to speak with the maids afterward, they could find help for Kellen.

"I bet it was the crown," Cecilia said, interrupting my thoughts. "Poor people always think the crown has more value than it really does."

"Of course it wasn't the crown," Porcia said. "It sits upon the King's head. What servant would be foolish enough to—"

"It wasn't the crown, miss. Nothing was stolen," the sergeant said.

Both Porcia and Cecilia turned to the man and blinked at him. I waited, watching to see if their guileless expressions would trick him into revealing more, but he remained silent.

"Girls, your oats are growing cold. Eat. I'm sure we will

learn soon enough why we were interrupted at such an hour."

We ate in silence for several long minutes, listening to doors open and close and furniture being moved about. Finally, the banging stopped, and footsteps descended the stairs.

"I do hope no one touched my delicates," Cecilia said ever so softly to Porcia with a shiver. "I could never bring myself to wear them again."

The sergeant cleared his throat uncomfortably and stepped back as the captain returned.

"Thank you for your cooperation," the captain said.

"Did you find what you were looking for?" Maeve asked, standing.

"No, ma'am," he said.

"Are you certain you cannot tell me? I might be able to—"

"Unless you practice magic, I doubt you can assist."

Cecilia gasped.

"You cannot use magic to find what's missing. It's forbidden."

Her performance was exceptional. She truly was Maeve's daughter.

The man held up his hands.

"We are not looking to use magic. We are searching for signs that it's been used."

"But magic can only be used by a caster or enchanter?" Cecilia echoed. "Why would you search here?"

Before the man could be pulled into her inane banter that would most definitely lead nowhere, I asked a question of my own.

"What exactly would a sign of casting or enchanting look like?"

His gaze flicked to me.

"I can't say, miss."

"Because you've been sworn to secrecy or because you don't know?" I pressed.

"Eloise," Maeve said calmly, "that's quite enough."

I quickly looked down at the table.

"I'm sorry, Mama," I said quietly.

"It's quite acceptable for her to ask, Ma'am. My niece was curious about the same thing. The less you know, the safer you are," he said. "I must ask, who is sleeping in the attic space?"

My heart stalled then jack-rabbited into a speed that made my hands shake. How could I have forgotten about Mother's books?

"I do, sir," I said.

"Why?"

I looked up, confused.

"Why?" I echoed.

Maeve chuckled.

"As you can imagine, if you have a niece this age, the girls want their own spaces. My Eloise was willing to sacrifice a few conveniences to have the whole attic to herself. I thought she was quite clever with her walls and sitting area."

The man's gaze held mine as Maeve spoke.

"Do you believe yourself to be clever?" he asked.

I could feel Maeve's gaze bore into me.

"That's an unfair question, sir. If I answer that I do, I will sound vain. No young lady wants to sound vain."

He smiled slightly.

"Very true. What happened to your cheek?"

"As you can imagine, stacking that furniture so high is not without its dangers. I haven't been to the market in over a week because of my foolishness."

He nodded. "Do be careful in your future, clever endeavors."

I inclined my head and went back to eating, grateful he hadn't discovered the books.

The man said his farewell and left me to endure Maeve's scrutiny. It was obvious she hadn't liked that I'd spoken at all. Unable to sit there in silence, I looked up and boldly met her gaze.

"I'm sorry, Mama. I didn't know what to say. I was afraid if I lied, he would know. I answered as truthfully as possible without implicating—" My throat closed, and I cringed.

She tilted her head at me.

"You were surprisingly adept at it."

Panic clawed at me as I realized what I'd done. I'd shown her how skilled I could be when answering her with the truth, but not the complete truth, as well. I said nothing, waiting for what she would do next.

"As the man said, you do have a clever mind, Eloise. It will be an asset to you if you use that cleverness appropriately."

"Yes, Mama," I said.

"What does it mean that they came here, Mama?" Porcia asked.

"That they know we're here," Cecilia said. "Why else would they be searching homes?"

"Perhaps it's just a precaution before our beloved prince arrives," Maeve said, looking at me.

"Do you think it wise to push the manservant for information so soon after the first search?" Porcia asked.

Maeve's cool gaze swung to her youngest.

"First?" I asked. It wasn't that I was trying to save Porcia from Maeve's wrath. Instead, I wanted to learn what I could. While I was unable to say anything before, perhaps I would find a time when I could speak. And when I did, I wanted to be able to say everything.

Maeve leaned back in her chair and tapped her fingers against the table, lost in thought for a moment. Then, she sighed and shook her head.

"Rather than speculate why or how often these searches will occur, girls, I want you to go to town and see what you can learn."

The girls immediately stood and left the room without finishing their breakfast. I took another bite of mine, not yet willing to give up my freedom for the day. Surprisingly, Maeve did the same. We ate in silence for several moments before Maeve pushed her bowl aside only half eaten.

"It's time," she said, standing. "Come Eloise, there is news."

Confused, I stood and followed her to the entry. She went straight to the mirror, kissed it, then spoke the words to wake it. Grimm's face slowly emerged from within the smoky expanse of glass without her asking to show him. Beyond him, I saw nothing but treetops. It appeared as if he was looking down at us. His expression brightened when he saw Maeve.

"My love, we've found the girl. As you said, she is in a cottage with seven small men. Miners by the looks of them. We're watching, waiting for them to leave. When they do, we will take the girl."

"Very good, Grimm. Thank you for your excellent work. Remember to watch the ribbon. Check it hourly."

Grimm's expression fell slightly.

"Forgive me, my heart. On our way here, I checked it constantly. During one check, the wind took the ribbon. I tried chasing it, but one of the beasts caught it, and I couldn't win it back."

Maeve glanced at me, her expression unreadable, before focusing on Grimm.

"Very well. Watch and continue to report to me."

She sent the mirror to sleep once more then turned to me. The silence grew as she studied me.

"The loss of the ribbon is unfortunate. However, don't mistake its absence as enticement to disobey me, or I will see Grimm beat Kellen far worse than the ones you've received. And, if you try to run and join your sister, I will have Grimm kill Kellen. Then, you will be returned to me by the very men who killed your sister."

I didn't doubt a word of her calmly delivered threat.

"You are mine. Do you understand?"

"Yes, Mama." I paused for a moment. "Does that mean you don't intend to bring Kellen home?"

"I'm sorry to ask for your patience a little longer, dear one. Grimm will ensure we reunite you with your sister."

Whether that reunion occurred when we were both alive remained to be the question.

"Now that we know Grimm is there, we will proceed as we discussed. Take the pig for a walk as you liked to do, and talk to Kaven. If you've not returned within the hour, I will use the mirror to tell Grimm you no longer wish to see your sister again. Do you understand?"

"Yes, Mama."

"Tell me what you really think, Eloise? Do you plan to run?"

"No, Mama. How did you know that Grimm was there with Kellen? And what would have happened if he had summoned you while the guard was here?" I asked, giving her one of my random thoughts to appease her.

"I can sense the mirror when it summons me. If I'm not here or unable to wake it, whoever summons me has to wait. The mirror will never reveal its nature unless I call upon it."

"Should I be worried about speaking with Kaven so soon after the search? Especially after how rude I've been to him?"

"Use that clever mind of yours, Eloise. Find out when the prince is due. You have an hour. Don't disappoint me."

I nodded and stood, eager to go outside no matter what the reason.

A few minutes later, dressed in a cloak and my sturdy shoes, I strode toward the woods, nearly dragging the pig along with me. He seemed oddly subdued, and I wondered if he had felt like a captive too, despite the walks Heather took with him.

"Please, Mr. Pig," I said softly. "Walk faster. I've been locked away in that house for too long, and she only gave me an hour."

The pig grunted and picked up speed. The oddity with which he seemed to understand me had faded in light of recent events. However, after my conversation with Rose and her obvious understanding about magic, I began to wonder what she might have done to the poor creature.

Elation filled me as another thought occurred. Rose had sensed the magic Maeve had been using near me. Perhaps the old woman would be able to help me find a way to free myself and the others without endangering Kellen. I only needed to find a way to get into town. And after that, a way to stop Maeve once I discovered what she intended to do with the prince.

Nothing a clever girl couldn't handle. I sighed and continued through the trees, letting the pig lead us off the trail as he snuffled and grunted with his nose to the ground.

But first, I needed to speak to Kaven and eat some crow. Not for Maeve's benefit but for my own peace of mind. I'd spoken so harshly to him because of my notions of his guilt. Granted, it hadn't helped that he had been surly and suspicious as well. However, I now realized how warranted his doubt of an unknown woman had been. I wished I had been more doubtful myself. Of Maeve. Of the messenger boy. Of everyone.

"The wasp has returned," a voice said from nearby.

Startled, I whirled around, dropping the pig's tether.

"No need to send your pig after me," Kaven said. He stood just behind a tree, his clear, deep blue eyes shifting between me and the pig.

"Is that fear I see in your eyes?" I said, unable to help myself.

He patted the tree and gave it a considering look.

"I wasn't sure I'd picked a tree large enough to stop the both of you."

I smiled, amused. He was likable now that I knew he wasn't evil. My humor faded as that thought reminded me of my purpose.

He noticed, and his answering smile faded.

"I thought you'd taken to avoiding the forest like you'd threatened to do the first time I met you."

"I've been unavoidably detained," I said.

"Does your detainment have anything to do with your bruised cheek?"

I lifted my hand to the cheek in question.

"After boasting of my intelligence, I would prefer not to talk about this."

He considered me for a moment then inclined his head.

"I will not mention it again."

"Thank you."

We stared at each other for a moment before I bent to fetch the pig's tether. The creature hadn't gone far, just a few steps away to snuffle the ground.

"You seem different," Kaven said, drawing my attention. "More subdued."

I gave a wry smile, thinking of all the things that were restraining me. A curse. Maeve's threat on Kellen's safety. The idea that Maeve might be watching me with her detestable mirror even now.

"That happens when one struggles with an overdue apology," I said smoothly.

His brows lifted.

"Apology?"

He looked right then left.

"I need to find somewhere to sit. I'm feeling faint."

I snorted and shook my head as he folded his arms and leaned against the tree, waiting expectantly.

"I'm sorry I hit you with the rock. It was unnecessarily forceful."

"And?"

"And I promise to use a branch next time."

He threw his head back and laughed, a dimple emerging on his cheek. I'd forgotten how handsome he was and didn't resent the way my middle did an odd flip at the sight of his humor. In fact, I embraced it and let myself desperately wish my life was currently on a different course. One that might involve him.

Gently tugging on the pig, I turned and resumed walking. Kaven quickly fell into step beside me.

"Is that what brought you out today?" he asked. "The need to apologize?"

"Don't flatter yourself. The pig was overdue for his walk. And I was eager for some sun on my face."

From the corner of my eye, I caught him studying me and glanced at him.

"What?"

"I'm still trying to understand you."

"Oh? I thought you were learning all my tricks," I said, remembering the last time we'd met and how he'd successfully deflected my blows.

"I believe I've barely begun to know you, Eloise Cartwright. But, I would like to."

His words sent a shiver of fear through me. This was exactly what Maeve wanted.

"That's a bit forward of you," I said primly.

He chuckled.

"You seem to appreciate forwardness."

"Sometimes." I stopped walking and faced him. "How long have you been with the prince?"

His humor fled, and mistrust crept into his gaze.

"Why do you ask?"

"I've lived here, on the King's land, my entire life. I want to know why."

The suspicion cleared.

"Your mother helped save the kingdom."

"My mother?" I shook my head and resumed walking. "My earliest memory of her is a day we went to the market. All the other women were walking briskly, buying what they needed. Mother did neither. She walked slowly, letting our maids haggle for better prices. She needed to sit and rest often and napped as soon as we returned home. How could a woman with no strength have saved the kingdom?"

"It's not strength that rights wrongs, Eloise, but determination."

I shrugged indifferently while storing that bit of information away. Determination I had in plenty. If what Kaven said was true about my mother, perhaps I was meant to follow in her footsteps and save the kingdom's Prince.

"Why are you out in the woods?" I asked. "Hasn't your errant Prince returned to ply you with work yet?"

"Are you trying to rid me of your pleasant company?"

"Hardly. My sharp words are good for you. As are menial tasks. Surely there are some princely soiled underthings for you to scrub by now."

Kaven snorted.

"I've never met a woman open to discussing the washing of underthings."

"Such topics are acceptable when speaking of royalty, didn't you know? One simply must know everything about the lives of our betters."

He gave me an odd look, a cross between concern and disappointment.

"You sound as if you hate the Prince. Have you met him before to carry such animosity?"

"Animosity? I hold no such strong emotion for our errant Prince. The best I can conjure is disdainful indifference. His drawn-out impending appearance has disrupted my life," I said before I could stop myself.

"How so?"

"Visitors come under the guise of condolences to press for information about his Royal Highness's return as if we know more than the common populace in Towdown. I resent the intrusion as it's a constant reminder of what was taken from me."

"I'm sorry, Eloise."

"It is what it is. Lowly people such as ourselves have no influence on the decisions of our betters. We can only live with the consequences of them. But if you do have the Prince's ear, please tell him to get his royal backside home."

"I will inform him that a beautiful damsel impatiently awaits his return. Perhaps it will hasten his progress. Unless you plan to greet him with a rock."

I rolled my eyes.

"I've already sworn off rocks."

Kaven grinned.

"Do you truly have nothing better to do with your time than torment me?"

He gave an exaggerated sigh.

"There are a few things that do require my attention today. Will I find you walking tomorrow, Eloise?"

"Only if you continue to wander the woods like an idle miscreant."

"You wound me."

I could clearly see that I hadn't.

"When you speak with your Prince, you might want to mention your apparent boredom. I'm certain he will help you correct it."

CHAPTER NINE

MAEVE STOPPED PACING BEFORE THE FIRE AS SOON AS I opened the door to the otherwise empty kitchen. Turning, she watched me remove my cloak, her face an impartial mask that worried me more than her false kindness. The kindness was a ploy to hide who she really was while she strove to manipulate those around her. However, this was the calm before the storm where she let her real nature show.

When I looked up from removing my shoes, she stood before me. Her hand lashed out and connected with my cheek with a vicious crack. The strike stung, but I knew well that it could have been worse.

"I returned straight away after speaking with Kaven," I said nervously.

"Speaking with him, Eloise? You insulted him the entire time."

I'd known she would watch. Yet, hearing her admit it made the entire conversation with Kaven repeat in my head. Because Maeve was unfamiliar with my prior relationship with Kaven, I could understand why she thought I'd insulted him.

"I flirted with him."

"That was flirting?"

"Yes. He smiled and laughed and liked talking to me enough that he hopes to speak with me again tomorrow."

She considered me for a moment, some of the suppressed anger leaving her eyes.

"Have you kissed a boy, Eloise?"

The question startled me.

"No, Mama."

She sighed. "Then, the fault in this failure is mine."

"Failure? But he seemed to trust me and said he would speak with the prince."

"He was making light of your comments, my dear. It's clear the boy has interest in you. However, you lack the knowledge to foster it. But, I think I have just the way to educate you regarding how to correct your approach. Would you like to go for another outing tomorrow?"

I had seen her parties and feared how she meant to educate me. Yet, I knew there was only one right answer.

"Yes, Mama," I said.

She smiled at me, her expression filled with pride.

"Then you will go with Cecilia to the Brazen Belle to learn how real flirting is done."

My brows rose in surprise before I could stop myself. I knew very well what the Brazen Belle was.

"Don't fret so. No one will know it's you, and I promise you're only going to observe. You're too precious to me to be used like Catherine and Heather."

"Mama, please. He already noticed I was acting differently despite my efforts to the contrary. If I start acting out of character even more so, won't he become mistrustful?"

She tilted her head and looked at me.

"What do you suggest?"

"Kaven sees me as a young girl who has no experience with boys. Let me continue as such for a few days and see where it leads. I don't know your purpose in determining when the prince arrives or understand your urgency, but what are a few more days when so many have been spent already?"

Maeve said nothing as she stared at me for several long minutes. The throbbing in my cheek increased with each beat of my heart, and I began to fear that I'd pushed too far and would quickly suffer more abuse. Yet, despite her assurance that I would not be used like Heather and Catherine, I saw our fates intertwining if I went to a whorehouse to learn about flirting.

"You say you want to be a young lady of good breeding but are doing nothing to show me that is your true path. A young woman of good breeding is adept at learning information and sharing it, Eloise. What have you learned?"

I remained silent, knowing I'd learned nothing of use to her.

"We need to know when Prince Greydon will return," she continued. "You have three days to attempt to innocently gain the information. After that, you will learn to embrace the power of your beauty and clever wit. You will acquire the skills that women with less refinement have honed over the years to gain everything they desire. And, you will use everything you have to obtain what we need by the night of the fifth day. Do you understand, Eloise?"

"Yes, Mama."

"I don't think you do," she said with soft menace. "But after a visit to the Brazen Belle, you will. Now go to your room. The sight of your face is a sore reminder of your failure."

I hastened to leave her presence.

In the solace of the attic, I wet a cloth in the cool water of my washbasin and pressed it to my abused cheek. My life hovered on a precipice. A single misstep, and I would find myself in far worse circumstances than my current one. How would I ever convince Kaven to share the Prince's plans with me?

Sighing, I sat on my bed and looked across at its empty twin. I missed Kellen's calming presence. I missed Judith and Anne. And above all, I missed Mother. She would have been amused by each encounter I had with Kaven. Except, perhaps, the one where I bashed him with the rock. But even then, she would have warned me to curb my temper by using that patient voice of hers. She would have never slapped me.

I snorted, realizing the fruitlessness of comparing Maeve's actions to that of my mother's. My mother would have never murdered anyone much less seen either of her daughters physically punished for anything.

The need to free myself from Maeve's influence drove me to set aside the cloth and carefully dig out Mother's herbology books. Without the lock securing the door, I didn't spend any time absorbed in their pages, but rather spent my time familiarizing myself with their content in general.

Every book had notes about potions or spells. Most had sporadic entries that intertwined with the use of common enough tinctures. A few contained pages dedicated to certain potions. One that caught my eye was a potion to change one's appearance.

"Eloise," Maeve called from below.

I startled and looked around wide-eyed before collecting myself.

"Coming, Mama," I answered as I quietly hid the books.

Lightly running down the stairs, I found Maeve once again waiting for me in the entry. She stood near the mirror, the image of Heather and Catherine moving about our kitchen fading from view. Dread pooled in my stomach. Had Maeve witnessed me with the books? Would she ask what I'd been reading? Would she demand to see them?

"Your sisters are returning. It will be good for you to greet them and hear their success."

I said nothing, too relieved she hadn't called me down to question me. Though, I did wonder how she knew they were coming—perhaps she watched them with the mirror too—and what she would do if they hadn't been successful.

Outside, the rattle of an arriving carriage ceased, and I moved to wait a few steps behind Maeve. Cecilia threw open the door, a pleased smile on her face.

"I can see you have news. Let's move to the sitting room. I'll ring for tea."

"Please, no more tea. Another sip, and I'll float away."

Maeve smiled at her daughter, artfully took her arm, and led the girl into the sitting room. I glanced at Porcia, who lingered behind like me.

Her gaze flicked to my cheek.

"What happened?" she asked.

"I spoke with the manservant, but he wasn't forthcoming with the information Mama wanted."

Porcia's gaze slowly swept me from head to foot. Her scrutiny bore no hint of any malicious emotion. Yet, her next words contradicted her expression, as they often did.

"You'll learn to do as you're told."

She walked past me, entering the sitting room not far behind Maeve and Cecilia. Knowing Maeve wanted me present, I followed. Once again, she patted the seat beside her, bidding me to sit near. Cecilia, already seated across from her mother, watched me closely, a slight smirk curving her lips as I did as I was told.

"Tell us what you've learned," Maeve said.

"Searches are occurring in every home within Towdown, including those on the outskirts, like ours. They began after Mr. Fletcher's carriage was discovered idly wandering the streets last night. All four occupants were dead, and the driver was missing."

"Why are they searching homes for signs of magical use and not signs of the driver?" I asked. It would seem logical to me to suspect the driver if the man was missing.

Maeve glanced at me.

"You've seen the results of a magical death, and the result of completely draining a person's life energy."

Images of Anne and Judith filled my mind, and I quickly understood why the guards were searching homes. Maeve focused on Cecilia once more.

"I had hoped that Mr. Fletcher and his companions would make it home to their wives before the spell finished its work. Any news of the others?"

Cecilia looked at Porcia.

"All are still alive as far as the gossips know though a few have been struck by some mysterious illness that keeps them abed."

"That is perfect," Maeve said. "A mysterious malady is just what we need to help deflect suspicion. Porcia, I will leave it to you to foster that notion. Did either of you manage to entice new patrons to our nightly gatherings?"

"Yes, Mama," they both said.

"Lovely."

THE BIRDS CHIRPED EXCITEDLY though their pretty songs barely penetrated my notice as I wove through the trees. With no pig to slow me, I quickly made my way toward the Royal Retreat as my mind raced, trying to find a solution to all of the problems that plagued me.

Last evening, Maeve had once again used Heather and Catherine to entice another group of dinner companions into her service. I doubted even now that the men knew they were under Maeve's thrall or that she had fed from them. She had made me stay through the initial invitation, a reminder of Catherine and Heather's place in Maeve's household. And, my future place if I continued to fail her. She'd excused me only after a warning that I had three days to learn the Prince's whereabouts.

The sounds of the men's satisfied groans and the wet licking still haunted me. But as much as I wanted to save myself from such a fate, I feared what Maeve planned to do with the Prince and how many more would suffer if she gained the information she wanted.

I needed to find a way to warn Kaven. Yet, with the curse binding my words and Maeve watching my actions, I didn't see how I could stop anything. The idea of doing what I was told grated at me. But I needed to keep Kellen safe. The image of the mirror rose to my mind, and I cursed its existence yet again. What I wouldn't give to destroy it. Perhaps then I would have a chance.

I wished Mother hadn't died. Although I wouldn't have wanted to subject her to Maeve's cruelty, I would have felt less lost if she were still with me.

"Going somewhere?" Kaven asked in amusement.

I whirled and realized I'd walked right past him. A smile played about his lips, flashing the dimple I found so heartwarming, and his eyes twinkled with humor. He wore the same hat pulled down to his ears, his darker hair escaping the confines. Suddenly, I itched to touch it and know its texture.

Grinning wryly, I smoothed my hands over my skirts and looked away for a moment.

"I was coming to see you."

"And yet you walked by as if I did not exist."

Blushing slightly, I looked up at him.

"I know very well you exist."

"What were you thinking with such singular focus?"

"I was wondering if my mother would approve of what I'm doing."

"Meeting a lowly servant in the woods?"

I snorted, turned, and started walking more slowly this time, picking a direction at random. Kaven joined me.

"I can hardly consider you lowly when you think so highly of yourself," I said.

He gave me a quizzical look.

"You believe I think highly of myself?"

"Most certainly. You accused me of trespassing when we first met, and after you learned who I was, you still knocked me off my horse, spanked me—"

"There is no need to list my transgressions. I remember them well. And I sincerely apologize for all of them. It's not that I think highly of myself but rather that I have a need to protect those I serve."

"It's admirable that you do," I said, understanding his need to protect those close to him. Heather and Catherine weren't my family, yet I still wanted no ill to befall them.

"Do you believe the Prince needs such ardent protection as to accost a girl in the woods?" I asked the question sincerely, no playful teasing in my tone. He glanced at me and exhaled slowly.

"Yes. Although I no longer believe you're a threat, the next girl may be."

I tilted my head at him.

"How do you know I'm not a threat? Perhaps I'm the biggest threat of them all."

He stopped walking and studied me. The way his gaze swept over my face and lingered on my lips set my heart racing.

"I think it would be wisest if I say nothing further," he said softly. "Lest you refuse to meet me again tomorrow."

I forced a small smile, my heart heavy. For the sake of the kingdom, Kaven needed to see through me.

"I'm uncertain if it's wise," I said.

"Why?"

"I still don't understand your reason for wanting to speak with me after all I've done."

He shrugged slightly.

"You're the most real woman I've ever met."

I couldn't stop the disbelieving noise that escaped me.

"I shall tell my friends that all it takes is a knee to the testicles for a boy to take them seriously."

Kaven chuckled.

"That it does."

We walked in silence for several moments.

"Aren't you going to ask if I sent your message to the Prince?" he asked finally.

"Should I?"

"I have it on good authority that girls are very interested in everything royalty does."

I grinned.

"Most girls might be. I'm tired of the constant princely chatter. Why is his life so much more important than ours?"

Kaven's brows rose.

"You don't believe it is?"

"No. He's a person like any other. The only importance his life has is that which we give it. If the Prince and I were alone in the world, why should I grant him authority over me? His birthright doesn't make him better than I am, only more known. Thus, all lives should hold equal value to his."

"Such talk could be considered treasonous," he said gravely.

"And that way of thinking only proves my point."

"How so?"

"Rulers come into power two different ways," I said, holding his gaze, needing him to understand the deeper meaning of what I was telling him. "Some are lifted up from the people by the people, such as our current royal family. The power they have now was once given to them because the people trusted the judgment of the first king. Other rulers come into power by taking what they want through coercion or fear. But both, in the beginning, started out as a person just like you or me."

"I understand how you would think the Prince's life has equal value to the common man," he said. "But I don't understand how my remark about treason helped prove it."

"The idea that any who disagrees with the Royal family's edicts are guilty of treason is a fear tactic to ensure the King remains in power."

Kaven slowly shook his head at me.

"I'm unsure if I should be impressed with your logic or run in fear that you're preparing to start a revolution."

My heart started to pound as I said my final piece.

"A little of both might be in order if men ever took women seriously."

I held my breath as I studied his serious expression, daring to hope he would understand who his threat was.

"Can I tell you something?" he asked.

"Yes."

"The Prince isn't like that. He's not one to subjugate his people. He's kind and wants to bring about a true peace again."

My hope withered and died.

"Can I tell you something?" I asked.

He chuckled.

"You always do whether I want you to or not."

"I don't want to speak of the Prince again. His existence has brought me nothing but pain."

Kaven bowed slightly, and we continued walking. I liked Kaven as much as I disliked him. Why didn't he read deeper into my words and hear what I couldn't come out and say? Frustration robbed me of further conversation, not that it was needed. Without comment, we walked a circle that took us farther from the Retreat and closer to my home.

"Thank you for today," Kaven said. "It gets lonely out here."

"Have you ever thought of leaving?" I asked. "Packing a bag and journeying to places unknown?"

"Have you?" He studied me intently.

"Every day since my mother died," I said softly.

He took half a step closer.

"I'm sorry for the pain you suffer."

I shook my head and looked away.

"Suffering is part of life. It's a journey we all endure until it ends. Better to suffer than to never exist. For between the sufferings, there are moments of great joy," I said, thinking of the family I had known. "We only need to see those moments for what they are and hold onto their memories during the times of trial."

He shook his head slightly.

"You are still a puzzle to me, Eloise. I wish I would have known your mother. To raise a woman such as you, she had to be something special."

"She was."

"Will I see you tomorrow?"

"Perhaps."

I left him in the trees, already doubting I would return. If he were wise, his loyalty to the Royal family would stop him from saying anything no matter how much he might trust me. And that was just as it should be.

When I entered the kitchen, Maeve was once again waiting.

"Nothing of importance again," she said.

"I did not insult him today."

"No. Instead you lectured him. However, your assessment of rulers couldn't be truer. I'm very relieved you see the current king for what he is, a weak man clinging to the remnants of power that never should have belonged to him. It's time for a change, don't you agree?"

Heart pounding with realization, I uttered the necessary words.

"Yes, Mama."

Maeve smiled and swept from the room.

Stunned, I looked at Catherine and Heather who worked quietly at the cutting board. Both wore twin expressions of fear. Seeing them helped solidify the truth of what Maeve had just let slip.

She planned to overthrow the King. But how?

For the sake of the kingdom, I needed to find a way to free myself from Maeve's control.

CHAPTER TEN

"LIFE RARELY GIVES ONE WHAT ONE WANTS," MAEVE SAID, patting my cheek consolingly. "Better to come to terms with that now."

I nodded, trying to quell the fear churning in my middle.

"You will not cause Cecilia trouble, will you?"

I shook my head.

"Good. Enjoy your outing. Do not return until after midday. I have guests I plan to entertain."

Maeve wasn't yet dressed, her thin robe leaving very little to the imagination, and I could guess what type of entertaining she would do.

She turned to Cecilia and handed her two vials.

"Drink them as soon as you reach the edge of town," she said.

Cecilia nodded, and my worry only deepened. Over the

last two days, Maeve's visits to town and my forced seclusion in the attic had allowed me time to read the books without fear of being watched. While I hadn't learned anything that would help me free myself, I now understood what those vials contained.

Maeve turned to me once more.

"When you return, you can take a nice walk before sunset to try your new skills. Learn well, Eloise."

I endured Maeve's hug then followed Cecilia outside and climbed up into the wagon beside her. I wore an old dress Maeve had given me. Cecilia did the same.

"Are you ready for an adventure, dear sister?" Cecilia asked.

I didn't answer, and she chuckled as she clucked the horse into motion. It didn't take long to reach the edge of town. Cecilia slowed the horse and lifted her vial to her lips. I hesitantly did the same, swallowing the potion that would change my appearance so no one would recognize me. Part of me was relieved. I didn't want anyone to know my shame after today. Yet another part of me wished everyone would see what was happening to me so someone could help.

A tingle spread over my face, and I looked at Cecilia to see her features waver and change. Worried, I reached up to touch my nose and brow. Everything felt the same to me.

"It's not truly changing you," she said. "That would take far too much power."

She pocketed the vials and clucked to the horse. I

watched the houses go by and tried not to think about what was to come. My time of innocence was at an end. The thought had barely formed when I realized that my innocence had ended long before this moment.

It didn't take long to arrive at the whorehouse. Cecilia pulled the wagon around back to a small stable and tossed a coin to the boy waiting there.

"Take care of the horse. We will be awhile," she said.

I followed her, fighting the urge to run. When Maeve had returned late last night and released me from the attic, she had shown me Grimm with Kellen in the background. Afterward, she had reminded me what fate awaited my sister if I disobeyed or tried to run today. The image of Kellen fast asleep in the sunny clearing steadied my resolve, and I entered the backroom of the Brazen Belle with determination that quickly faltered.

Although I'd seen Kellen naked before, and more recently, Heather and Catherine, I was unprepared for the general state of undress in the Brazen Belle's less public room. Women walked around with the tops of their dresses low enough to show their nipples, or worse, completely around their waist so their breasts were fully displayed. The men who lingered in the room watched with avid interest as the women moved from group to group, speaking to the men as if at a social gathering.

"Sit and watch," Cecilia said, leading me to a cushioned chair off to the side near a set of stairs. "Study how the women approach the men. They need to entice them to get them up to the private rooms with them. That is how they get paid. Do not move from this spot. I will return."

My eyes widened as I realized she planned to leave me. I reached for her, but she laughed and twisted out of the way.

"Don't be a child, Eloise. And do not look away or fail. If you return to Mama as ignorant in the ways of men as you were before, you know what will happen."

I wanted to claw Cecilia's laughing eyes out of her head as she walked away. Instead, I faced the room and did what I was told.

It didn't take long to see that the most successful women were the young ones who played coy...even if their breasts were bared. The pattern was simple enough. The woman smiled at a man and glanced away quickly to get his attention. Once he approached, she spoke softly as would a nervous maid. He would say something, and she would nod and take his hand. Occasionally, he would touch her breast as he spoke but not always. The older women were less sought after but did have some success with bolder tactics such as stepping in front of a man and placing his hand on her breast or under her skirt.

I was so engrossed in my study, I didn't notice someone sat beside me until a hand settled on my skirts just above the knee.

Heart hammering, I looked at the man and narrowed my eyes.

"I am not coy, and I am not for sale," I said plainly. "Be gone."

The man frowned but left to find more willing quarry. Feeling sick and afraid, I returned to my study.

"How's the pig?" a familiar voice asked.

I swiveled in my chair to look up at Rose. The old woman watched me with a small smile. My eyes immediately began to water. The potion hadn't fooled her. She knew it was me.

Her expression changed to one of concern.

"You didn't eat him, did you?" she asked, sitting beside me. "If you did, I won't be angry. A bit ill, but not angry."

"No. Mr. Pig is well enough. It's you that brings tears to my eyes. I'm relieved you know me for who I am."

She tilted her head at me, a small frown creating even more wrinkles in her brow.

"Why hide who you are but feel relief when someone sees through the spell?"

I opened my mouth but nothing came out. I didn't try harder, too afraid Maeve would notice my attempt to speak freely.

Rose's eyes narrowed on me.

"Someone cast these spells on you, haven't they?"

I remained mute, giving no indication of truth in her words. Yet I felt unrestrained joy. Someone finally knew. She might not know it was Maeve who cast these spells, but at least she knew I was bespelled.

The old woman sighed and sat back in her chair, looking out over the room.

"Wipe the tears from your eyes, child. Whatever trouble you've gotten yourself into will likely only grow worse if you're found crying to me about it."

I quickly wiped my eyes and pretended to go back to studying the room.

"I know about spells to keep a person silent. I've used a few myself."

That admission worried me. She saw it in my expression and grinned.

"Don't worry. He deserved it. The beast had a tendency to lose his temper and yell at me. I'm not a woman who takes kindly to that sort of treatment."

One of the women on the floor walked up to us.

"Rose, you'll scare away the customers. You were told to stay in back."

"She's helping me," I said quickly. "I need to learn how to capture a man's—"

"I know why you're here," the woman said. "What good do you think an old woman's words will do you? Her twat dried up ages ago and hasn't seen a cock since then."

"Do you think cocks have evolved into something more mysterious than they were in my day?" Rose asked with a cackle. "Suck it or fuck it, it's the same result. A happy man willing to give up a little of his coin. There's no mystery in this business."

The girl glared at Rose and walked away. The old woman stared after her.

"Cocks might not have changed," she said softly. "But much in Towdown has." She glanced at me. "I find it odd that she knows your purpose here, and I do not."

"Why do you find that odd?"

She shrugged slightly.

"Like you, I'm unable to say much. Capturing a man's interest is easy. Are you sure you want to do that?"

I almost answered that I didn't. Then fear stayed my tongue instead of the curse. What if Maeve was watching? What would she do to Rose?

The old woman shook her head at me.

"Your fear is answer enough. You need help, but can't ask for it. And I can't help without understanding the full problem. We're in a bind, aren't we?"

I turned away from her, focusing my attention on the women once more.

"I wonder if they all know I'm watching," I said. "Do you think their behavior would change if they knew they were being observed?"

There was a long moment of silence beside me.

"Everyone's behavior changes when they know they're being watched," she said finally.

"Yes. It does."

"How is the pear tree by your mother's grave?" she asked.

I felt a pang and hoped the bird still sang to Mother in my absence.

"I'm not sure. I haven't been for a long while."

"You should go speak to the dead about what you cannot speak to the living. And stay true to yourself, Eloise. Many young women lose their way by not staying true to themselves." She glanced around the room, an indication of exactly what she meant, then patted my knee and left.

Her words stuck in my mind as I spent the next several hours in the chair. My backside had long since gone numb by the time Cecilia returned.

"We need to go now."

She didn't wait for me to stiffly get to my feet but hurried toward the door. I struggled to keep up and emerged to see the boy bringing the horse from the stable.

"Hurry and there's another coin in it for you," she said.

The boy quickly hitched the horse to the wagon, and Cecilia tossed him the promised coin as she clucked the beast into motion. We left the yard of the Brazen Belle just as my nose began to itch. I lifted my hand to scratch it, but she swatted my hand away.

"It's not real. Don't call attention to yourself."

I kept my hands clenched in my lap as she wove through the streets. The tingle stopped by the time we reached the outskirts and started on the path that led to our home and the Retreat.

"Do you think anyone noticed us change?" I asked.

Cecilia gave me a cutting look.

"If they did, we wouldn't still be in the wagon. We would be in a cell under the palace. I don't know why Mama continues to show you favor. You're unintelligent and not worth her consideration."

I sat quietly in the wagon for the rest of the journey home, my anger simmering. I didn't want Maeve's consideration or Cecilia's misguided jealous hate. I wanted them both gone.

Cecilia pulled the wagon to a stop before the shed in too little time and hopped down before Hugh even appeared. The main doors of the house opened, and Maeve stepped out, fully dressed.

"Welcome home, my darlings." Her gaze lingered on me as I climbed the steps. "Did everything go well?"

"Yes, Mama," Cecilia said, kissing her mother's cheek. "Eloise studied the entire time."

"How would you know?" I asked. "I didn't see you after you left me in the common room."

Maeve's gaze pinned her oldest daughter.

"You left her?"

Cecilia's smile faltered.

"I was never far, Mama."

"We will discuss this later. Leave me."

Cecilia cast a hateful glance my way before hurrying upstairs.

"What did you learn?" Maeve asked.

I repeated my assessment of what the younger whores

did to see the most success and the bolder practices of the older whores.

"There's no need for the latter," Maeve said. "I think that may test the boy's trust in you."

"Yes, Mama."

She tilted her head at me.

"Why did you tell on your sister?"

"You said you wanted to know what I was thinking, and I disliked how she treated me on the way home."

"Oh? And how was that?"

"She said I wasn't intelligent enough to warrant your favor or consideration."

Maeve smiled slightly.

"You proved her wrong, didn't you?"

I couldn't help the smile that tugged my lips.

"I did."

"I hope it was worth making an enemy of your sister. Even Porcia hasn't been foolish enough for that. Now go upstairs and change into something more suitable. I believe you need to take a walk."

Maeve's warning about Cecilia didn't give me a moment's pause. Cecilia could do no worse to me than Maeve herself. Hurrying upstairs, I quickly changed into one of my mourning gowns. When I returned to the foyer, Maeve nodded her approval.

"You will do well. Go. Gain the information I seek and truly win my favor."

With my nerves dancing in my stomach, I left the

house.

I found myself on the path to my mother's grave without consciously intending to go there. It made sense though, given the anxiety plaguing me. Birds flitted between the trees, their songs beginning to soothe the rough edges of my emotions as I walked.

When I arrived in the clearing, I barely recognized the place. Moving to the bench Hugh had made for Kellen and me, I sat and looked up at the pear tree in awe. Its branches were thick with leaves that rustled in the early spring breeze. Blossoms still dappled the greenery, their sweet scent perfuming the air. I couldn't see any fruit yet but knew it was coming quickly, given the speed with which the tree had grown.

The bird who always sang for me while I sat by Mother's grave started singing, its little eyes watching me. A sense of peace settled over me, and I exhaled slowly. Remembering Rose's words, I whispered a quick plea.

"Please don't let Maeve hear me."

I watched a pear blossom fall slowly to the ground as I considered what to say.

"I'm sorry it's taken me so long to return. Life's been difficult since you left. I regret not seeing the necklace for what it was." My next words died in my throat, the curse preventing me from saying it was Maeve who killed her. Frustration welled within me that I couldn't even speak freely with no one around.

"You wanted so much more for our lives than what we

have now," I said angrily. "I hate that our choices have been taken from us. But don't worry, Mother. I'm doing as you asked. I'm watching over Kellen and keeping her safe as best I can."

I tilted my head back, letting the sun warm my face.

"I'll do what I must, but I fear the consequences if I'm successful. I wish you were here to guide me."

The breeze drifted by, caressing my cheek as if my mother were indeed there and trying to comfort me.

Lost in thought about what I needed to do next—find Kaven—I remained where I was. For Kellen's sake, I couldn't refuse to do as Maeve asked. For the Prince's sake, I knew I should try to ruin my attempt. Yet, Maeve had made it clear that failure again wasn't an option. I silently wished there was a way to break her mirror. Without that and the ribbon, Kellen would be safe.

"Lost in thought again, I see," Kaven said.

He walked through the trees, approaching from the direction of the Retreat, and stepped into the clearing.

"At least this time, you aren't wandering the woods."

"How is it you always seem to find me?" I asked as he crossed the space to sit beside me.

"It's a question I often ask myself whenever I'm looking for you." He glanced at the pear tree where the little bird still sang. "The wildlife is louder around you."

I followed his gaze to the tree, ignoring his teasing smile.

"You didn't cut it down."

"I couldn't."

"Thank you."

I sat beside him for a moment, trying to work up the courage to give him a coy glance.

"You seem quieter today," he said. "Is something troubling you?"

"I'm struggling against a fate I cannot change," I said. "Each morning, I open my eyes and feel more frustration and anger than the day before. I can no longer see what is good in my life. Instead, I only see the bad."

I looked at him, meeting his troubled gaze.

"So much has been taken from me. When will it stop?"

His blue eyes held mine as he reached up and gently touched my cheek. I felt comforted and something else. Something more than I'd ever felt with a boy before. I licked my lips and tilted my head up. His gaze dipped to what I offered. His fingers gently tugged on a loose curl. I saw something shift in his eyes. A primal, deep emotion that set my heart racing. He leaned toward me, the fingers of his free hand touching mine. The simple contact warmed me better than any winter's fire.

My lips parted as anticipation and a heady mix of yearning shivered through me. At the last moment, he stopped.

"Eloise, I...I'm sorry. I cannot."

Embarrassment coursed through me, and heat flooded my face. I knew what I needed to do next. My palms grew sweaty at the thought of placing his hand on my breast.

I swallowed hard and pulled my hand from his.

"No, I'm sorry. Forgive me." I kissed his cheek lightly then bolted. He called my name, but I didn't stop running until I neared the house. Relief and fear warred inside of me. I'd done what I'd been told and failed. The kingdom might be safe, but I was not.

Steps slowing, I entered the kitchen. Maeve was there, waiting calmly at the table while sipping her tea. She set the cup aside when I entered.

"Where were you?" she asked.

"In the clearing," I said, confused. "With Kaven like you told me."

She studied me, giving nothing away.

"And? Did you discover when we can expect Prince Greydon?"

"No, Mama. I failed," I said, holding her gaze. "But, I don't understand how. I had his attention. He stared at my lips just as the men at the whorehouse had with the women they liked. But he didn't kiss me or whisper in my ear. Instead, he told me he couldn't."

"Couldn't what?" Maeve asked.

"I don't know."

Her eyes narrowed, and she tapped her fingers against the table. I waited for her to unleash her fury, hoping she would use me as a target and not Kellen.

"Innocence is a burden," Maeve said. "Tomorrow, someone with more knowledge will accompany you."

I PACED THE CLEARING, anxious to have my second attempt over and done. Cecilia stood near a tree, not far away, not that I could see her. The potion she'd used had changed her appearance to blend with her surroundings.

Despite her presence, the bird in the tree sang for me. Its song echoed among the trees. It didn't take long for Kaven to appear, and I was grateful for the tiny creature's help.

"I wasn't sure you'd return," he said, not approaching me.

"I'm still not sure I should have," I said.

"Eloise, I'm sorry if I hurt you."

I crossed the clearing so I stood toe to toe with him.

"You cannot hurt me," I said. "You can give me something much better."

I boldly grabbed his hand and lifted it to my cheek.

"Tell me you want nothing to do with me, and I will return home."

"I cannot," he said thickly.

"Then tell me what you do want from me."

His gaze dipped to my lips again, and Cecilia's presence faded from my mind as his free hand gently captured my arm. He tugged me closer to him. Close enough that I could smell the pine on his clothes from so much time outdoors.

"I want more than I can give in return," he said softly.

Taking his hand, I slowly slid it down my throat to my breast. My heart raced under his palm.

"I'm not asking for anything in return," I whispered.

He groaned, a tormented look crossing his face.

"Eloise, you tempt me to forget my purpose and forsake those depending on me to stay vigilant." His hand curled into a fist under mine, and he slowly withdrew.

"I beg you for your patience," he said. "When the Prince returns—"

"And when exactly will that be? It seems everything in my life now centers around the wayward Prince's return," I said hotly.

Kaven's expression turned more aggrieved.

"I cannot say when for I do not know. Forgive me."

Shaken, I whirled away from Kaven and struggled to guess what his lack of knowledge meant for me.

"I'm sorry, Eloise," he said again.

When I turned around to tell him to toss his apologies, he was already gone. Angry and afraid, I left the clearing. Cecilia fell in step beside me, the spell fading as we moved.

"He was delicious to look at, Eloise. For your sake, I do hope Mama gives you another chance at him. I imagine he would be remarkable between the sheets. I have half a mind to try for him myself." She made a humming sound. "I doubt it would do any good, though. He was interested in what you were offering. No doubt there. Yet, he refused. What a waste."

Her words, though vile, gave me hope that Maeve

wouldn't be too upset about yet another failed attempt. However, as we drew closer to the house, I couldn't stop doubting that Maeve would allow me any more chances.

"How did it go?" Maeve asked, her gaze shifting between me and Cecilia when we entered the kitchen.

"He refused again," I said.

"Of course he did," Cecilia scoffed. "He clearly wasn't interested in what you were offering. Any fool could see that."

My mouth opened in shock, and I turned to Cecilia, anger clouding my eyes.

"How can you say that? You saw him."

"I did indeed. Can you deny that he fisted his hand after you brought it to your breast? Or that he left moments after you demanded to know when the Prince would return?"

Her lips curled in a small smirk, her gaze holding mine. "You can see by her silence it's true, Mama. So much time wasted."

I wanted to—something hit my back. The blow robbed me of breath and brought me to my knees. Before I could comprehend what had happened, another blow hit me, landing across my shoulders. I cried out and fell to my hands and knees.

"You've brought this upon yourself," Maeve said, her voice marked with anger.

I looked up just in time to see the wooden rod she used on the mirror fly toward my head. I lifted an arm, sparing myself from a direct hit. But my arm went immediately numb from the blow, and I collapsed to the floor. Strike after strike rained down on me. It seemed never ending, each one adding to the accumulating pain until I stopped feeling.

Maeve threw the rod aside.

"Leave her as she is. Do not help her. Do not comfort her. Cecilia, you and Porcia will go to town immediately. Starting today, we will entertain every night. See there is a group for each day of the week. I'm done waiting patiently. It's time we move forward."

I couldn't fear what was to come or pity the men. I could barely think beyond each painful inhale.

The door closed behind Maeve. A whisper of noise, the brush of cloth against stone, penetrated my awareness.

Gentle lips pressed against my cheek, and I imagined Mother kneeling over me, her gaze filled with worry and love.

"Tattling never goes unpunished," Cecilia whispered in my ear. Her hand came down on an exceptionally damaged spot as she pushed to her feet.

I hissed in agony.

"Never cross me again, my sweet sister."

CHAPTER ELEVEN

Time floated by in a haze of semi-awareness. At some point, Heather told Catherine she was having pain in her knee and asked her to brew some of the tea that had helped me. When Catherine finished, she set the pot and cup on the hearth near my head. I knew what they were doing and worried they would find themselves in my place. Yet, I couldn't refuse the help.

I struggled to roll to my side then to lift the pot with my good arm. Much of the liquid slopped outside the cup. When I did manage to fill it, I shakily brought it to my lips and gulped the tepid contents. With no strength left, I collapsed to the floor and groaned at the contact of hard stone against my tender flesh.

The tea slowly began to work its magic, and I realized that this beating wasn't any worse than the previous ones. In a few ways, it was milder. My head wasn't fogged, and my face wasn't swollen. Most of the damage was to my back.

I briefly considered going to my room but rejected the idea. The tea was down here. As was food and water. So I remained where I was on the floor and slept while the tea kept me numb.

Raucous laughter woke me well after the sun had set. I lifted my head and groaned softly in pain. The kettle and pot were where I'd left them, and I helped myself to more tea. As the numbness settled over me like a warm blanket, awareness rose. Men were in the dining room. Based on the laughter and sounds of pleasure, so were Heather and Catherine.

I closed my eyes against my failures and drifted off again.

The next several days passed in the same manner. Tea, sleep, and dinner parties. Gradually, I weaned myself from the first two and plotted against the latter.

When I could move without pain, I bathed and returned to my room in the attic. My mourning dresses had been ripped to ribbons, which I didn't mind. However, all of my other dresses had been ruined as well. Angry, I stared at the one dress that remained, neatly laid out on my bed. It was a maid's dress.

With nothing else clean to wear, I put it on and bundled the soiled dress so it could be laundered. The next morning, I appeared for breakfast, determined to take my place at the table. I didn't want to be there. I needed to be. I needed to know what had happened during my time in the kitchen.

Only Maeve sat at the table, quietly eating a soft-boiled egg.

"Good morning, Mama," I said.

She turned in her seat to look at me, her welcoming smile fading.

"You've decided to stop trying to be the daughter I need, then?"

"No, Mama. My other dresses have been ruined. This was all that was left for me to wear."

A slow smile curled her lips, and she chuckled before gesturing to the chair beside her.

"I warned you not to cross your sister," she said. "You will need to find a way to earn her forgiveness. When I have time, I will have other dresses made for you."

"Yes, Mama," I answered as I sat. "I apologize I didn't discover what you wanted. The boy did finally reveal that he couldn't tell me because he didn't know."

"Ah." She reached out and smoothed back my hair. "However, knowing that does not make me regret your punishment. You failed me too many times. When I ask you to do something, it doesn't matter how it gets done, only that it does. Do you understand?"

"Yes, Mama."

"Good. Now, put the boy out of your mind."

"What would you like me to do next, Mama?"

Her gaze raked over me.

"Since you're dressed like a maid, you might as well act like one. Go help Heather and Catherine for the day." She waved her hand, dismissing me.

Heather and Catherine looked up when I entered the kitchen. Both had dark smudges under their eyes and gave me weary smiles.

"It's good to see you up," Heather said.

"It's good to be up. Cecilia destroyed all my dresses and left me this to wear," I said. "And since I look like a maid, Mama sent me in here to help you two. You look in need of rest. Tell me what to do and go nap."

Heather immediately shook her head.

"We cannot. We disappointed Lady Grimmoire last night, and she told us we cannot sleep until we redeem ourselves."

"How did you disappoint her?"

They shared a look.

"We refused something one of the men wanted."

I frowned, unable to imagine what they would have refused when they'd already done more than I'd known to do.

"Don't worry about us," Catherine said. "Come help us roll out this dough. We're hoping to make this a dinner she won't forget."

THE SOUND of many hooves racing into the yard

interrupted our efforts less than an hour later. Heather quickly wiped her hands and headed for the door. She returned not long after with a vial.

"You're to take this," she said. "Lady Grimmoire wants you upstairs making beds when they search."

My heart lurched as I understood what was happening. The King's Guard had returned. I uncorked the vial and drank the contents then hurried up the back staircase.

Footsteps echoed from the main stairs as I ducked into Cecilia's room, the closest to me. I didn't know what Maeve expected from this trickery but knew better than to hesitate to follow her instructions. I'd just started making Cecilia's bed when one of the guards entered the room. I looked up from my task and felt a jolt of surprise. It was the sergeant who'd endured Cecilia and Porcia's inane prattle during the first search.

"Step aside, miss," he said without a trace of recognition.

I moved away from the bed.

"Where are the young ladies of this house?"

"I don't know, sir. I'm sorry."

"Don't be. Please join your mistress in the dining room."

I glanced at the unmade bed, wondering what I should do.

"You can return to your task after we're done."

I nodded and left the room to join Maeve. She wasn't alone. The captain stood near the door, watching her while also watching his men move about the room. They looked in the sideboard, under the chairs, under the table, behind curtains...one even stood on a chair to check the candle holders in the overhead chandelier.

"This is utter nonsense," Maeve said from her place at the table. "You've already searched our home."

She glanced at me when I stepped farther into the room.

"Now what?"

"The guard sent me to you, My Lady," I said with a small curtsy. "He said I could finish my tasks once they were done."

"Sit," she said with a wave of her hand before returning her annoyed gaze to the captain. "Next, you'll be telling my kitchen staff to stop working."

"I truly apologize for the inconvenience. We are conducting our search as quickly and as thoroughly as possible."

"Yes. You are. I'm only struggling to understand why you did not do so the first time so you need not have returned."

"I assure you that we did do a thorough search. However, we've been ordered to do so again."

"I heard from my aunt's sister that bodies keep turning up dead," I said with false timidity. "She thinks it's a plague."

"Nonsense," Maeve said dismissively. "If it were a

plague, the King wouldn't order our homes searched. You still believe it's someone using magic, don't you?"

"I cannot say, Mistress."

Maeve snorted.

"Mama?" a concerned voice called from the entry.

"In here my darlings," Maeve called.

Cecilia and Porcia entered, looking suitably concerned about the presence of the guards. Neither spared me more than a passing glance. However, I noted them well. Cecilia was wearing one of my dresses, and Porcia one of my hair ribbons. I hoped one of the guards pissed in my lovely stepsisters' beds.

"What's happening?" Cecilia asked.

"Another search," Maeve answered.

"I beg your pardon, Mistress, but where is your other daughter?"

"I sent her away. Given her curiosity regarding magic, I thought it best to distract her with other interests until everything is resolved. No mother should be separated from her child. I hope this situation resolves itself quickly."

"As do we all," he said.

One of his guards entered just then and said they'd searched the house and found nothing. I breathed a sigh of relief that I'd taken more care to hide my mother's books. Although at first glance they seemed innocent enough, I didn't want to risk anyone discovering them. Most of all Maeve.

"Thank you again for your time and patience."

Maeve nodded as the guards left. Once the door closed behind them, she looked at the girls.

"How many?"

"Sixteen so far," Cecilia said.

She tapped her fingers on the table.

"Good. Taking less from the new groups is preserving them."

"However, there's a rumor circulating that all the dead men were at the same gathering," Porcia said nervously.

Maeve's gaze flicked to Cecilia for confirmation.

"Just a few houses. The wives noted the men were absent on the same nights."

Maeve closed her eyes, taking a calming breath.

"We will need to cancel tonight's gathering and rearrange the others to reduce the chance of more clever wives noting the same thing."

"Yes, Mama," Cecilia said before turning toward me. "You look so different, dear sister. The potion suits you. Do you like my dress?"

"I'm surprised you would lower yourself to wear second-hand clothes. Perhaps if you stuff it a bit," I glanced pointedly at her chest, "it will fit you more attractively until Mama can have your own made for you."

Maeve laughed.

"Eloise, please tell Heather and Catherine there will be no need for a large dinner tonight."

Dismissed, I left the room.

AFTER SEVERAL DAYS avoiding the solace of the woods, I could no longer stand the pattern that had taken hold of my life. Waking, eating, pacing the confines of the attic, then finally going to the kitchen to offer my help to prepare the evening meal had taken its toll on me. As had the nightly parties.

I could no longer count the number of times I'd considered running. However, I was no closer to discovering Maeve's purpose or a way to break the mirror. With the mirror intact, Maeve would catch me before I found help and Kellen would bear the brunt of the punishment.

Restless, I descended from my self-imposed prison and went in search of Maeve.

"She and the girls went to town. She said she would be back before dinner," Heather said when I asked.

I itched to do something drastic. To make a run for it. To try to break the mirror. Anything. But fear and Heather's knowing gaze held me in place.

"Did she leave any instructions for me?"

"Only that if we allow anything to happen to you, it would cost us our lives," Catherine said quietly.

"But our lives are already forfeit," Heather added before turning away to resume her cooking.

At some point we'd all given up hope that Kellen would rouse an army to come rescue us. Not when she couldn't even manage to rouse herself. In every glimpse of her that I'd had through the mirror since she'd left, she always slept. And I worried for her.

"The sun and trees call to me. If Mama arrives, please let her know that I've taken the pig for a walk on the estate grounds. I'll return within an hour."

Catherine nodded acknowledgement, barely looking at me. I knew they doubted my words.

"I will not abandon you or my sister," I said before leaving.

Outside, the spring wind had warmed slightly and caressed my cheek in welcome. I inhaled deeply, letting myself feel a grain of hope in my unexpected, if temporary, freedom from Maeve's ever watchful gaze.

Mr. Pig greeted me at his gate.

"Ready for a walk?" I asked him. I quickly tethered him and led him away from the shed since I wasn't sure where Hugh was lurking. As soon as we were in the trees, I spoke softly to the pig.

"You helped me once before. I need your help again, now. Find me something I can use to break her mirror."

The pig let out a nervous squeal and sidestepped.

"Come now, Mr. Pig. If we don't stop her, who will? We both know what will happen if she continues. You saw the results of her efforts as well as I did. Now is our chance. We may not have another."

The pig grunted and put his nose to the ground. I walked behind him, watching and waiting for him to root up something astounding. An enchanted sword, preferably.

Instead of finding a miraculous weapon of some kind, he wandered into my mother's clearing and snorted at the pear tree. I looked at the heavily blossomed tree, fighting against the hopelessness weighing on me. Rose had hinted the pig was special. He'd found my friends when asked to find something more. Instead of asking him for help, maybe I should have asked Rose.

"I thought you were my friend," I said, removing his tether. "Go. See how well you fare in the world. The size you are, someone is sure to butcher you within a day."

In frustration, I threw the tether to the ground. The pig grunted then squealed and ran back toward the estate. I had a feeling I would find him cowering in his pen.

"You speak to him as if he can understand you."

The sound of Kaven's voice startled me, and I turned to glare at him.

"I speak to all animals as if they can understand me because I think they might. There are beasts in the Dark Forest that can speak, are there not? It would be foolish to assume only we are the intelligent ones."

He held up his hand in a placating manner.

"I meant no affront. It was only an observation." He cocked his head, studying me for a moment. "Why are you dressed as a maid?"

"Why are you here, Kaven? To ply me with more

longing stares? Well, I'm not interested. Be gone. Leave me in peace."

"Eloise, I..."

I whirled around, looking for a rock or something else to throw at the knave. I found a branch and snatched it up. Before I could turn back to him, steely arms wrapped around my waist, locking me in place. The pressure of his chest against my back sent an enjoyable shiver through me. I railed at fate for its cruel reminders of the life I should have had. One where I was free to flirt and discover men at my leisure. Instead, I knew only their baser side.

"Release me or suffer," I hissed at him.

"I didn't mean to hurt you," he said against my ear.

My anger intensified.

"Accidental or intentional, pain is pain." I attempted to stomp on his foot, but he widened his stance.

He growled in my ear and released me. I spun around, ready to wield the branch. We glared at each other, neither moving.

"Fine," he said finally. "I'll leave you be. For now."

"Forever, you ass."

I swung the branch, but he twisted out of the way.

"Names won't change how you feel about me, Eloise. When you're calmer, you'll realize that."

He turned his back on me and stalked away.

"I look forward to our next meeting and your apology."

I screeched and threw the branch at his head. He

ducked at the last minute. His laughter taunted me until he disappeared from sight.

As I stood there panting, body shaking with the need to chase him down and hurt him, I realized he wasn't the one I wanted to hurt. The latest beating I'd received was because of Cecilia's lies, not Kaven's cluelessness. But in the end, the blame for every pain I'd suffered fell to Maeve. And the anger I felt now was at my impotence to stop it from continuing.

"I hate," I whispered. "I hate so deeply it chokes the breath from me."

The breeze swept through the sunlit glade, washing over me with the light scent of pear blossoms. Rose's words not to lose myself suddenly echoed in my mind.

"Is there anything else to lose?"

I gave the pear tree and Mother's grave one last look then turned away. My steps were heavy on the way home, and my mind so occupied with dark thoughts that I didn't at first hear the impatient stomp of a horse's foot or the collective jangle of livery. When I did, I stopped just at the edge of the trees.

In the yard, another contingent of the King's Guards' horses waited. I bit my lip, understanding the house was being searched again and looked down at my dress. I couldn't go in there. Not without a potion to hide my face. Not with Maeve's lie about sending me away.

"Lies," I said softly to myself.

A rabbit bolted from its nearby warren and froze to look at me.

"Nothing good will come of this," I said to it. Then I turned to hurry away only to bounce off the chest of one of the guards.

"I think you're right, miss. Nothing good will come of this." He reached for me, and I ducked away, panicking. If he took me inside, the captain would see me and know. He would have questions I couldn't answer.

I tried to run but the guard caught me from behind.

"Do not struggle," he warned.

I didn't listen. I rarely did.

He hit me, his fist connecting with the side of my head. Dazed, I wondered how many blows one could suffer before one's intellect became affected. When I couldn't remember why I'd been hit, I decided I'd already suffered one blow too many.

The guard lifted me over his shoulder and carried me out of the woods.

"Tell the captain I found a maid in the woods who tried to run. I'm taking her to the castle."

My world spun again as I was tossed upon a horse, and a rider swung up behind me.

"I'll let him know."

"But I have to stay here," I said, my words slurred as a wave of dizziness pulled at me.

Something tickled the side of my face, and I absently lifted a hand to wipe away my hair. My fingers touched moisture, and I looked in curiosity at the red staining my hand. The man behind me clucked the horse into motion.

By the time we entered Towdown, my head throbbed fiercely. But my thinking had cleared enough to reconsider my circumstance. The guard had me. I couldn't say anything to incriminate Maeve. But I could tell the truth about who I was. Perhaps they would then question Maeve about her lie. Would it be enough to point suspicion at her for the deaths though? Probably not. Was it worth risking Kellen's safety to take the chance?

Ahead, the castle spires towered over the rooftops. I'd never been this close to the castle and would have preferred to keep it that way. As soon as the guard slowed from a gallop at the castle gates, I spoke in a rush.

"I'm Eloise Cartwright. I live at the estate. This is a mistake."

"Quiet," the guard said sharply, maneuvering the horse at a trot to veer toward the side stables, away from the grand front stairs.

"It's the truth," I said desperately. "Ask Lady Grimmoire. She will tell you."

"And do all young women who live at estates on royal land wear the clothes you do?"

I looked down at the plain, serviceable dress that most maids were known to wear. He dismounted and grabbed my waist as another guard jogged toward him.

"My other gowns were ruined." He plucked me from the saddle and gripped my arm, leading me toward the side door. "Ask Kaven about me. He's the manservant who is preparing the Royal Retreat for the Prince's arrival. He'll tell you."

He paused, sharing a look with the other guard.

"You seem to know a lot about what's happening at the Royal Retreat."

"Yes. You see? I live there."

"Or you've been watching it for a long while."

My growl of frustration was cut short with his next words.

"Take this one to the dungeons," the guard said. "We'll get the truth from her when the captain returns."

Fear consumed me.

CHAPTER TWELVE

I STOOD IN THE DARK CELL, STARING AT THE SHADOWS THAT danced beyond the bars. The single torch in the passage didn't illuminate much inside the space in which I'd been thrown, and for that, I was grateful. Something scurried to my right, making me glad I was standing. I hadn't dared to sit for fear of the dank straw that littered the floor.

Time passed, measured only in the replacement of the guard. I shivered lightly and kept my hands away from the cut on my head, too afraid of contaminating it any further. I already worried what falling into the filth once had done.

Somewhere nearby, metal groaned against metal. Footsteps echoed, growing closer, but I did not approach the bars to look.

"Bring her," a firm voice said.

I trembled and clasped my hands before me. When the

guard appeared, I did not move until he opened the door. He and another man stepped in.

"I will come with you willingly," I said, hoping to avoid more bruises.

"Good," the first guard said, grabbing me anyway. The second covered my head with a smelly sack, robbing me of what little vision I'd had. Together, they tugged me forward. I stumbled, and their holds bit painfully into my flesh.

After several steps, they turned me. Light began to twinkle through the gaps in the coarsely woven material. I shifted my head, trying to see, and caught a glimpse of a man standing a few steps in front of several others.

The guards stopped me and forced me to my knees. I winced at the hard stone that dug into my shin.

"You were caught fleeing from royal lands. What were you doing there? Who are you?" a voice demanded.

"I swear to you, I am Eloise Cartwright. I live at the estate from which I was taken."

There was a low murmur of voices, then some of the light was extinguished.

"Remove her hood," the voice said.

The coarse material was lifted from my face. I blinked once against the dim torch light and focused on the man who stood before the rest. He wore the regalia of a prince from the fitted coat and ruffled cravat to the shiny black boots. His brown eyes swept over me before he glanced at the men behind him. Those closest were illuminated enough to see they were the wizened men who likely guided the Prince.

"Why did you run?" the guard asked.

"I was embarrassed to be caught wearing this dress."

"And why are you wearing it?"

"My other dresses were ruined."

The Prince made an impatient sound.

"Do not waste my time with the trivialities of a woman's wardrobe."

He nodded to a guard, and the man turned and slapped me. The crack echoed in my ears and stung my cheek. Some of the men, those hidden by the shadows, shifted as if uncomfortable with my treatment. Little did they know I'd suffered far worse.

I lifted my head, disdain in my eyes for the prince before me.

"If you don't want to hear about women's dresses, then don't ask about them."

There was a gasp and a chuckle. The Prince turned to glare at those behind him before focusing on me.

"You speak boldly for someone in my dungeon."

"I speak boldly because I know I've done nothing to warrant this treatment."

"How did your mother die, Eloise?"

I thought of the amulet, and my throat constricted.

"Why does anyone die? Because their bodies fail them in some way. My mother was weak for a very long time, and it only grew worse as the years passed. I believe your father knows something about that. You should ask him."

There was a collective gasp this time.

"Your mother's name is known by the Crown. Yours is not."

"Odd, considering I live on royal lands."

"Enough! You waste my time."

"And you waste mine," I said.

The guard slapped me again so forcefully my head turned. I swallowed hard and slowly straightened.

"You dare rebuke me?" the Prince asked.

"I dare," I agreed quietly. I lifted my head to look at him once more, my voice rising. "As the sovereign heir, it is your duty to protect the weak and the innocent. And by the rumored body count, I would say you're failing quite miserably. Open your eyes, Your Royal Magnificence, before you lose your kingdom."

"That sounds decidedly like a threat."

I couldn't disagree with him, but I didn't know what else to say to make him understand that the true threat was still waiting to be discovered.

There was another murmur behind the Prince, and one of his shadowy advisors stepped forward to whisper in his ear.

"What do you know of magic?" the prince asked.

"I know that it exists and that the King believes some of his people are dying because of it."

"Do you know why they are dying? Do you know the purpose behind these attacks?"

I snorted.

"I hope you have a better way to determine the guilty, Your Royal Benevolence, than questions that will only be answered with stout denials."

"Explain yourself," the old man said.

"If you believe me to be the person responsible, how do you honestly think I would answer? I would claim my innocence just as ardently as any innocent person would."

The Prince stared at me.

"My advisors are whispering behind me, debating your innocence for various reasons. Why should I spare you?"

My throat tightened around the words I raged to say. I lowered my head and took a few quietly wheezing breaths to calm myself. When I lifted my head again, I had the sense they were all watching me.

"Because I'm not afraid to show that I'm angry."

He gave an exasperated sigh and looked over his shoulder. The murmurs of frustrated old men rose.

"Explain," one voice said.

"I'm angry my mother died. I'm resentful that my father left, and my sister is gone. I hate the turn my life has taken. Look at me. I'm in the damn dungeon. But why would I hold the Crown responsible for what's happened to me? Except for this last part. To what purpose would I want to kill innocent people when I know the agony of loss myself?

You will spare me because I have no reason to do whatever is being done."

There was silence as the Prince considered me.

"What if I told you your mother's death was the fault of the Crown?" he asked softly. "That she sacrificed her vitality to save the kingdom, and that was why she was so weak?"

"I would tell you that sounds like the woman I knew. Her body was weak, but her convictions never were. Not once did she show a hint of blame toward the Crown for the life she lived. Neither will I."

"Where are your father and sister? Why did they leave?"

"I wish I knew where they were," I said, truly pained. "I'd like to believe my father left to escape his grief. I've never seen a man love a woman so completely as he did my mother. It hurt him to see her failing strength over the years."

"And your sister?"

"She escaped to escape," I said with a helpless shrug.

"Release her," the Prince said with a negligent wave of his hand. "She's no more than a foolish girl in the wrong place at the wrong time."

I scowled at his back. Foolish girl? He wasn't more than a handful of years older than me.

"Pompous brat," I said under my breath.

The guard to my right cuffed me upside the head.

"Watch your tongue," he warned before hauling me to

my feet. He held me in place as the Prince, the men in the back shadows, and the advisors left. Once the room cleared, the guard led me out a door and marched me to the side gate like some unwanted beggar.

With a shove, he forced me from the castle grounds just before dusk. Stumbling a few steps, I righted myself and glared back at the closed gate. That could have gone worse. However, it also could have gone much better. I recalled the conversation and came up with a thousand ways I could have answered differently. Regret clawed at me that what I'd said hadn't helped the Prince or his men see the threat to the kingdom was in my home.

Turning a slow circle, I got my bearings and started toward home. In the fresh air, a sharp odor slowly penetrated my nose. It took a moment to realize I was smelling whatever filth coated me. At the first well, I drew a bucket of water and tipped it over my head. Blood and grime ran down, staining my bodice. It took three more buckets to rinse away the worst of it enough to start the journey home.

Had I given the situation more than a passing thought, I would have endured the smell and waited to bathe when I reached home. As it was, walking home in a wet dress just before the sun set proved a very chilling experience. I shivered and rubbed my arms long before I reached the edge of town more than an hour later.

The cold and shivering didn't help the pain in my head, either. The steady ache increased to a pulsing throb. My anger grew with my pain. In the dark, I stumbled often on some hidden object as I made my way along the road leading to the Retreat. I clenched my teeth and found solace in imagining myself hitting the guard who took me from my home on a horse but failed to return me. Then I imagined hitting that ass of a prince.

I smiled slightly to myself at that image.

"Such a thing would only see me imprisoned again. But oh, what a lovely thought," I said to myself, staggering slightly on the road that seemed determined to never end. I could barely see my hand before my face and only knew I remained on the road because of the rut I followed. Then it suddenly ended. I turned a slow circle, trying to see where I might be.

A rumble came from overhead, and I looked up in annoyance.

"Could this get any worse?" I said to myself. Perhaps a flash of lightning would—

"That depends on your definition of worse," a familiar voice said.

The lightning I'd hoped for flashed just then, and I saw Kaven standing not far from me. Behind him towered the Royal Retreat.

"Bloody hell," I muttered as the light faded.

"Lost your way, my little wasp?"

"Obviously. It's darker than a—"

"No need to continue that thought," he said with a chuckle. "You look in need of assistance."

Another rumble sounded overhead.

"Not at all. I just need to wait for another bolt of lightning to show me the way." I tipped my head up to the sky, waiting, and gave a frustrated huff when nothing happened. Turning, I smacked my head against something, bruising my lip.

Kaven grunted. Lightning flashed, illuminating his chest inches from my face. I tipped my head back to glare at him.

"What are you doing?" I demanded, wincing at the taste of blood on my lip.

"I was going to help you inside."

"Inside the Retreat? Are you mad? That is the last place I would want to go. Prince Greydon is a royal ass. I can see why you like him."

Kaven snorted. Rain let loose just then, soaking my face.

"Come inside, Eloise," he said.

"Just turn me in the direction of home."

"Why is help so often rejected when it is needed the most? I saw the blood on your temple and watched you stagger your way up the drive. Let me help you."

I huffed in defeat.

"Fine. You may—" He scooped me up into his arms and started walking toward the house.

I stared up at him in astonishment. He caught the look and grinned in another flash of lightning.

"I'm feeling a bit of surprise, too. I'm not sure if it's you or the dress, but you're heavier than I expected."

I sputtered. "I am not heavy."

"If you'd like to remove the dress when we reach the Retreat, I'd be happy to try again."

I smacked the back of his head.

"Walk in silence, manservant."

He laughed and kicked open a side door that led us into a fire lit kitchen. I scowled at the drawn curtains. Had they been open, the light from the fire would have helped guide me on my own.

Annoyed, I turned my head to look up at him at the same time he bent to set me down. Our faces collided with surprising force. I gasped in pain against his mouth, my damaged lip protesting against the contact, and jerked back. He stared at me, his expression unreadable.

"I sincerely hope this doesn't count as my first kiss for I can only take it as an ill omen for any future romantic endeavors," I said.

He eased me to my feet, saying nothing as he moved to put more wood on the fire. I looked around the large kitchen in awe.

"What happened to you?" he asked.

I turned to look at him. His gaze swept up from the bottom of my soiled dress to my face. He frowned at whatever he saw.

"When I left you, you were angry but undamaged." He

reached out and gently moved some of my hair away from my temple.

"This is the doing of your kind Prince. Doesn't every ruler who wants to bring about a true peace terrorize his people?"

"Eloise," he said in warning. "Tell me what happened."

"There was another search on the house. I panicked and ran."

"Why did you panic?"

"Look at me, Kaven. Am I dressed like a young lady of good breeding? No. And just as I suspected, when I tried to tell the guard who caught me who I was, he didn't believe me. Because I tried running, they automatically assumed that I'm some evil enchantress killing the magnanimous subjects of Towdown and threw me in the dungeon."

"That doesn't explain the cut on your head."

"The guard hit me to subdue me." I grinned slightly. "It seems it's not in my nature to go quietly."

"Eloise..." He surprised me by gently pulling me into his arms and hugging me. He was warm and smelled clean and good. More than that, his embrace emanated a level of comfort and concern I'd longed for since Kellen disappeared. Unable to help myself, I leaned into it, resting my forehead against his chest.

"Why must life be so difficult?" I whispered.

His hand ran over the back of my head, smoothing down my back. I shivered. Whether from his touch or the cold, I couldn't be sure.

"There is no way to say this without sounding coarse, but you must remove your dress. You'll never warm while wearing that sodden mess."

I slowly drew back and looked up at his face.

"There's no need for me to warm," I said. "I'm close to home. I'll rest a bit then find my way."

"You are infuriatingly stubborn," he said, sighing.

"It's my best quality."

He chuckled and released me. Taking my hand, he led me to a chair. I sat with a sigh and closed my eyes, letting the fire's warmth wash over my face.

"I'll return in a moment," he said freeing my fingers.

I shivered in the chair as the heat from the flames slowly penetrated my clothes. Steam rose from my bodice. I would be lucky not to fall ill after this.

A scrape of noise announced Kaven's return. I didn't turn to look at him, too tired to move. Something soft brushed against my face. I opened my eyes to look at him. His gaze remained focused on my hairline, which he washed with meticulous attention for several long minutes.

"It's a small cut," he said finally. "It bled a lot, though. If you're determined to return home, I'll hitch up a—"

"No," I said firmly, pushing his hand aside. The idea of him coming face to face with Maeve sent a lance of panic through me.

"I'm fine. I only needed to sit for a moment. I can make it home now."

"Eloise, it's raining. Please let me take you home."

"The last time I saw you, I asked you to leave me in peace. The time before that, you asked for the same."

"That's not what I—"

"Your precise words matter little. Your intent does. Focus on your obligations, Kaven, and I will do the same." I stood, my legs and head protesting.

Kaven's gaze narrowed on me.

"You can barely stand."

"What I can and cannot do is not your concern. I apologize for the unintended intrusion. The storm made it darker than I'd anticipated. I can find my way from here." With a brisk nod, I moved to the door, determination giving me strength.

Kaven followed me closely. I thought there would be another argument as I stepped out into the rain, but when I looked back, his steady gaze remained impassive as he watched me. I turned as regally as I could, lifted the sodden mass of my skirts, and started for home, grateful for the flicker of light from the open door.

The damned dress weighted my arms, making them burn with strain by the time I left the circle of light. I plodded along in the dark once more. If not for the occasional crack of lightning, I might have missed the gap in the trees that marked the path to my home.

Turning up the drive, I could think of nothing else but the warmth of the fire, and felt relief when I finally spotted dim light through the trees from the windows. My numb fingers trembled as I let myself into the kitchen. The fire crackled merrily in the hearth.

I shuffled in, dripping on the floor. A gasp brought my attention to Catherine and Heather. Their eyes were wide as they stared at me for a moment then rushed to me. Their hands made quick work of the dress, stockings and shoes. As soon as I stood in nothing but my transparent underthings, they moved me toward the stool by the fire.

"Sit," Catherine said. "I'll fetch a blanket."

She hurried from the room.

"You should have stayed away," Heather said softly. "You should have saved yourself."

I frowned up at her, the look in her eyes making my stomach twist with worry.

"The guard took me," I said through chattering teeth.

"I know." She smoothed a hand over my hair then went back to her cutting board.

The door opened, and Catherine hurried back in. No blanket weighted Catherine's arms, and fear filled her gaze. She joined Heather, neither working, only watching as Maeve entered the room followed by Hugh.

I hadn't seen him in too long. He looked gaunt now, sickly.

"I thought you were truly gone," she said softly.

My heart stopped.

"Kellen," I whispered.

Maeve smiled slowly. My anger boiled, and I clenched my fists.

"As I said, I thought you were truly gone."

As I held her gaze, thinking that I could now strike out at her, I realized it was a test of obedience. A test to see how far she cowed me. Maeve wasn't foolish enough to remove the one thing that kept me under her thumb. Regaining control over myself, I hid my ever-present anger under my mask of indifference.

Maeve's smile vanished.

"Please do tell me what happened, Mama," I said calmly. "I love Kellen too much not to know. Afterward, we should discuss what happened while I was in the King's dungeons."

She studied me for a moment.

"You test me?" she said softly.

"No, Mama. I remain your obedient daughter."

Her regard turned cold and calculating.

"Obedience can be broken with the right methods. Strip. I want to see what they did to you."

My gaze flicked to Hugh who watched me as well. Then Catherine and Heather.

"Is there a problem?" she asked.

"You once asked if I wanted to lead the life of a proper young lady. Should a proper young lady bare herself to a man not her husband?"

"Should a proper young lady question her mother?"

She nodded to Hugh, and he advanced on me.

"I'll do it," I said quickly.

"Too late," she said.

Hugh grabbed the front of my shift and ripped it from my body. However, before the material gave way under his force, it cut into my skin. I bit my abused lip to keep from making a sound and quickly covered my bare breasts.

"Hands down, Eloise. I want to see."

Swallowing hard and turning my head to stare at the flames, I held still as Hugh yanked my thin underclothes from my hips. His breath skimmed my belly as he bent forward, and I wanted to whimper against the offense.

"Step away, Hugh," Maeve said.

Her heels tapped on the ground as she circled me. Her finger trailed along my lower back, and I fought not to shudder at the contact.

"They barely touched you," she said. "It's hard to be sure if your unmarked state is because the spell held and you could say nothing or if you found a way to quickly implicate me to save yourself."

"I said nothing to implicate you," I said when she stood before me once more.

"I have to be sure," she whispered, stepping back with a smile.

Hugh stepped forward, his eyes glinting green.

CHAPTER THIRTEEN

HATE, LIKE LOVE, HAD AN INFINITE CAPACITY. IT WAS A SIMPLE truth that I discovered as I lay before the fire during the next several days, unable to move or see clearly. Catherine and Heather, forbidden from helping me, proved through small kindnesses that they weren't completely under Maeve's control unlike Hugh, who despite his wasted appearance, had used his unchanged strength to bring me low.

Yet no matter how many times he'd struck me as I related my tale of my time in the dungeon, I'd managed to withhold one tiny bit of information. I said nothing of the Prince. In my story, he was just another man among men who had questioned me.

A log fell in the fire, sending sparks drifting up the chimney. It reminded me of the stars, a sight I hadn't seen for far too long.

Standing shakily, I made my way to the door and walked out barefoot into the night. The cool air felt good on my bruised skin as I walked down the dirt lane to the path that led to the overlook. I sat near the edge, tucking my skirts around me since I wore nothing but the maid's dress.

The stars shone brightly over the castle. It was a beautiful sight, but it didn't touch me. Nothing could. The raw hate I felt for Maeve wrapped around me like a protective cloak. I clung to it desperately, for I knew what waited in the shadows of my mind. Utter despair and resignation. It whispered that jumping from the cliff would be a fine end to a pathetic life. That there was nothing in my power I could do to change the course of events except to choose the time and place of my own death.

A branch snapped behind me.

"What gave me away?" I asked softly.

"The owl. Did you not hear it?" Kaven asked.

I focused on the night sounds and did, indeed, hear the treacherous creature.

"It seems I'm offensive to man and beast alike," I said.

I could feel him coming closer.

"It was me in the house that day," I said. "I saw a picture of a beautiful woman with a green necklace. Was she the Princess?"

"She was."

"How did she die?" I asked, already knowing the answer.

"She fell ill shortly after marrying. At first, those closest to her thought it was nothing more than sickness from traveling. Then she grew worse. Healers were called. No one could determine the cause."

"But you know, don't you? That's why you asked if something or someone new appeared before my mother's death."

"Yes. I believe it was the necklace, which was given as a wedding gift to protect her and lost after her death."

A necklace that had been sent to my mother by Maeve. Why? And why kill the Princess with it?

"Why would someone want to hurt the Princess?"

Kaven sat beside me, looking out at the castle with me.

"It's rumored that years ago, long before the King married his late wife, Queen Sevil, there was another woman. She tried ensuring the King's love with spells and potions. She wanted to be queen. To become a power of reckoning. But she failed and fled. Not for long, though. Strange things started occurring several years after Aftan wed Sevil. Shortly after that, Queen Sevil died and King Afton decreed that, if he should ever marry again, the people should rise up against their new queen. Peace has held Drisdall since that day."

I let the story settle in my mind, trying to understand his point.

"I'm too tired to be clever," I said.

He chuckled.

"Then why are you out here?"

A hand brushed my cheek, and I winced.

"Look at me," he demanded.

I turned my head and stared at him in the moonlight. Enough days had passed so that the swelling was gone. But even the dark could not hide the discoloration below my eye.

"What good is looking at me? You cannot undo what's been done. Only time can do that."

"Eloise, I'm so sorry."

"Why? You didn't hit me."

"When I saw you that night, I didn't realize how bad it was. I should have never let you walk home unescorted."

Bitterly, I turned away once more and looked at the stars. Why could no one see what was happening within my home? For a brief moment, I considered pressing the issue. However, the memory of Anne and Judith's bodies dissuaded me. No, it was better that he thought the guard had done this to me. I would not give him any hint of my circumstance that might endanger him, too.

"Make it up to me by finishing your story," I said.

"It's not a story but history. And the Royal family believes it is repeating itself."

"They believe an evil caster is going to try to marry the King? Wouldn't the people still rise up against her?"

"Not the King, but Prince Greydon, heir to the Crown and currently unwed."

"Oh," I said as my mind raced.

While younger women frequently married older men, I

didn't often hear of the opposite. Could Maeve's intention truly be to marry Prince Greydon? It made sense of her single-minded focus regarding Prince Greydon's arrival. But surely she couldn't think it would work when she was already known to the King and the King was protected from her influence by an amulet of his own. How did she think she would get the King to agree? The potions to change her appearance didn't last that long, and by her own mouth, a spell to change her appearance would be too costly.

No, she was far too clever to repeat her mistakes. If she failed once, she was going to try something else. But what?

"Why all these questions?" Kaven asked softly.

"So I understand why I'm suffering. So I can decide if protecting a prince is worth this price."

He gently wrapped an arm around me, likely intending to give me comfort; however, he only caused pain. I hissed out a breath and eased away from him.

"I'm deeply sorry for what they did to you. I'll speak to the Prince about the treatment of those they bring in for questioning."

"He's doing what he must. I should go," I said, getting to my feet.

He quickly stood and helped me up. His hand lingered on mine, warm and strong as he held my gaze. I wanted to lean into him. I wanted to beg him to help me. But most of all, I wanted to spare him from enduring Maeve's tormenting attention.

"How many have died now?" I asked.

His gaze darkened, and he glanced at the castle once more.

"Twenty-four."

"The deaths have slowed then."

"But not stopped."

"Stay safe, Kaven. Your life is worth as much as the Prince's in my eyes." I leaned up and gently brushed my lips to his cheek before slipping from his hold and walking the path home.

When I opened the door, Maeve was there. I said nothing to her as I poured myself a cup of water, which I drank before sitting by the fire.

"Where were you?" she asked.

"Looking at the stars, trying to remember why I cling so desperately to this life."

She stepped close and ran her hand over my hair.

"To protect your family," she said softly.

"Is that what I'm doing?"

Her hand stilled on my head. I didn't regret my words. To my very soul, I was tired of the games we played.

"If you've forgotten, perhaps I need to remind you."

"If that is what you wish." I stood and resumed my spot on the floor. "I'm ready."

She stood over me in silence for several long moments.

"Rest, my sweet Eloise. Tomorrow will be better for you."

She left the room, and I closed my eyes, tears finding

their way down my cheeks. If Maeve said tomorrow would be better, I would surely suffer some new form of torture.

I SMOOTHED my hand over the soft skirt of the dress as the seamstress made small sounds of satisfaction. Behind me in the mirror, Maeve watched me closely.

"Does the dress suit you, Eloise?" she asked.

"Yes, Mama." The words fell flat. Not ungrateful or disrespectful, only wooden. I didn't trust the new dress or Maeve's benevolence.

"Poor darling. I can't imagine the terror you felt when the horse reared."

I nodded politely to the seamstress, keeping the pretense of the story Maeve had given to explain the fading bruises covering my body and my need for an immediate dress. It was a new seamstress, one who had no knowledge of my previous need for mourning gowns. One who was discreet and wouldn't spread the tale of my injuries.

"Can you have another one like this ready soon?" Maeve asked.

"Of course, My Lady."

"Very good. I'll have someone fetch it once it's complete. Come, Eloise."

I stepped down from the hemming stool and followed Maeve from the shop. Hugh waited nearby with the carriage.

"Take us home," Maeve said.

The idea of returning to that hell so soon fed the despair eating at me. Maeve noticed as I took my seat.

"Perhaps when we return, you would like to take the pig for a walk," she said.

"Yes, Mama." I turned to look out the window, pretending not to notice her frown.

"You're too spirited to be broken, Eloise. Kellen, yes. But not you. Dispel whatever plagues you, and act like a proper young lady should."

"I'm not sure I know that role anymore," I said softly. "Is it laying bloody and broken before a fire? Listening to the maids suck the cocks of our male dinner guests? Cleaning away soot and ash?" I turned my head and looked at her. "I haven't been a proper young lady in a very long time, and I truly don't believe that's what you want from me. It's only presentation and appearance that matter, after all."

She smiled slightly.

"There's my clever girl. When we return home, take the pig for a walk. Spend some time outdoors. I will require you at dinner again tonight."

I nodded and resumed my study of the passing homes, dreading what would happen once she stopped her act of loving stepmother.

When we pulled into the yard, I went straight to the pig's pen and let him out. I didn't bother with a tether.

"It's time for a walk, Mr. Pig."

He ambled along beside me as I made my way around the house to the trail that led to my mother's grave.

"Don't eat any of the flowers in the clearing," I said just before we reached it. "I don't think they're natural and don't want you to fall ill."

The pig grunted and veered slightly to root around between the trees. I stared after him, frowning. The old woman's words about casting a spell on a beast came back to me.

"Are you truly a pig?"

The pig's head jerked up and swiveled to look at me. He started squealing and grunting in earnest, and my stomach dipped.

"Were you once a man?"

His head bobbed, and I felt sick. Like me, he too had been cursed. Again, the conversation with Rose came to mind, and I thought of her promise that she'd only cursed those who deserved it. Is that how Maeve viewed my curse? That I'd deserved to be struck mute?

It was only then that I thought of Maeve and the mirror. I hoped she wasn't watching. For if she were, the poor man would surely soon be dead.

"Hush," I said softly. "We will both suffer if you make too much noise."

The pig fell silent and followed me to the bench. I sat on the wooden surface, and the pig lay down nearby. We were both quite stuck in our current circumstances.

Sitting in the sun, I felt the spring breeze caress my skin

while the birds sang. The peace of the glade soothed the ragged edges of my frayed hope. However, when I left several hours later, I didn't feel more renewed but rather more bitter at the invisible shackles that prevented me from righting the wrongs that had been done to so many.

The pig followed me meekly back to his pen.

"I will try to find a way to speak to her," I said softly, thinking of Rose.

The pig squealed and ran to his shelter. I wondered if he feared Rose as much as I feared Maeve.

Leaving him, I let myself into the kitchen and found Heather and Catherine hard at work preparing another dinner feast.

"Can I help?" I asked.

"No, miss. Your mother gave strict orders that you're to do nothing to help prepare this meal."

I sighed and looked around the kitchen. It was on the tip of my tongue to apologize again, but I knew doing so would change nothing.

"Thank you for all the work that you do," I said instead then left the room.

Upstairs, I again started reading the book Mr. Bentwell had held for me per Kellen's request, wasting time until Maeve called me down for dinner.

I sat through the meal, detached from the conversation while still appearing every bit Maeve's attentive daughter. If Maeve noticed something amiss, she didn't comment. Once

Catherine and Heather appeared for their true part of the feast, Maeve dismissed me.

Seeking the haven of my attic sanctuary felt wrong while Catherine and Heather endured so much to feed Maeve's ever increasing need for power. Yet, I retreated without protest. There was nothing I could do for them.

While I passed through the hall, my gaze landed on the mirror. It was the key to setting Kellen and me free. How did one break an unbreakable mirror, though? And even if I found a way, how would I survive Maeve's wrath because I knew I wouldn't leave Heather and Catherine to suffer in my place.

Once more in my room, I stared out at the stars through my tiny window, pondering the answers to those very questions.

The following days mimicked the first. The pig and I would go to the clearing and sit there in silence for hours. Near dinner, I would return to wash and prepare myself. I would eat, speak when spoken to, then retreat to the safety of my room and Kellen's book of tales.

Another dress appeared at some point, laid out on Kellen's bed. I changed when needed. Bathed when needed. Ate when needed. I became a hollow replica of my former self as the bruising faded completely.

"Eloise," Maeve said, setting her spoon aside at breakfast one morning. "You haven't been yourself for the last week. What is the matter with you, child? Are you ill?"

"Has it truly only been a week?" I asked absently. I took

a small bite of oats, playing with my food more than eating it.

Maeve huffed.

"Honestly, Eloise, I think I might take you to a healer if you don't start acting yourself soon." Her tone, so filled with motherly worry, had me looking up at her. Her face was a complete mask of true concern. I stared at her, wondering if she was starting to believe her own lie.

"I'm fine, Mama," I said automatically.

She studied me, the look of worry never leaving her face.

"Would you like to go to town with Hugh to pick up supplies?"

"No, thank you. I upset Hugh when I'm with him."

Maeve frowned slightly.

"What do you mean? Has he hurt you?"

I almost howled with laughter at that.

"He scolds me to stay close when all I want to do is roam the market like I used to."

She considered me for a moment.

"Very well. Go to town with Hugh. Have your freedom for today. I think you've well learned the price of disobedience."

"Mama," Cecilia began, sounding annoyed.

"Quiet," Maeve said sharply. "I believe Eloise's melancholy is due to boredom and envy. The pair of you leave to visit with others daily while she's trapped here with nothing to entertain herself. Eloise knows what is at stake if she attempts anything. The spell is firmly in place, and Grimm awaits my call should the need arise. And I will be watching."

She studied me while she spoke, and I unflinchingly returned her gaze. I didn't allow myself to feel a shred of hope because I might be able to roam Towdown. There wasn't much I could do there anyway but pretend I was free. As she said, the spell held me even if my loyalty to my sister did not.

"Go," she said with a nod. "Fetch Hugh so the two of you can return before dark."

"Yes, Mama." I rose and left the room.

Hugh wasn't happy when he learned he was to take me to town and set me free while he was there. Like Cecilia, he dared to voice protest. Also like Cecilia, he was put in his place.

"Need I remind you all that Eloise has already been on her own for a day? The day she was taken by the guard. Nothing has happened since. The spell is effective. Do not question my judgment again."

Duly reprimanded, Hugh drove me to town in silence. I roamed the market, looking at vendors' goods and buying nothing. A few people stopped me to offer their condolences. Many just nodded hello.

As I mingled with the people in the market, I felt a connection, not just to them but to all the people in Towdown and Drisdall. They knew nothing of the danger that lurked in their midst. Naïve, they went about their days as if they had an infinite amount of them. Yet, my heart hardened when I overheard how many had died in the same unusual manner as Judith and Anne. Well over forty now.

"Your mother wasn't...shriveled when she died, was she?" one woman asked in a hushed voice.

I knew it was fear and not the need for gossip that had prompted her to ask such a tactless question. Reaching out, I placed my hand over hers.

"My mother was sick for a very long time. She did not die in the same manner as the men and women who have died since then."

She nodded and gave my hand a squeeze.

"It relieves me that your house has been spared."

"Not entirely spared. There was a misunderstanding during one of the raids, and I was taken to the castle's dungeon for questioning."

She covered her heart as she stared at me in horror.

"Oh no. Whatever happened?" I explained about wearing a common dress and running in embarrassment.

She tsked in sympathy.

"Men don't understand such things. You poor dear. I've heard there've been many women taken for questioning. They are not treated well in the dungeon."

Even as she said that, a contingent of guards made their way through the market sending many of the people scattering.

"My husband is considering moving to the North," she

said. "I hope he decides soon. I heard the guards are doubling their search efforts. They've been to our home twice already this week. Once in the middle of the night."

"What are they looking for?" I asked although I already knew the answer.

"Signs of magic. Why now, after all these years, I do not know."

I left her stall and returned to Hugh. The journey home was quiet, and Maeve waited by the door, a large smile on her face.

"I must send you to town more often," she said, descending to give me a large hug. I returned it, playing her game because I was too beaten down to fight it.

"You did well, speaking to so many and reminding them you are fit and content with life. It's useful to know how many have been discovered dead and that the searches are increasing in frequency."

She led me inside where a tea tray waited in the sitting room along with a new book.

"I thought perhaps you'd enjoy reading until dinner."

I picked up the book and found it was the type I liked. Maeve rarely seemed to miss any detail. It was a wonder she hadn't realized there was something amiss about the pig.

"Thank you, Mama," I said sitting.

She left me to read, calling me just before the first of her guests arrived. We'd just closed the door after greeting the last arrivals when a thunder of hooves rose outside. Maeve cursed softly and hurried me to the dining room.

"It would seem that the guard is here to ruin our merriment. Not a word about anything untoward that happens here." As soon as she spoke the command, the men's eyes flashed green.

"Heather," she called. "Please get the door."

Heather emerged with a nod and rushed to answer the knock at the main door. The Captain of the Guard followed her back into the room. He looked around in surprise.

"My Lady," he said with a bow. "I apologize for interrupting your gathering. We must search your home again."

"Do what you must. Warn your men to wipe their feet this time. Last time, they created extra work for my staff with their neglect."

"I will see to it." He looked over his shoulder and nodded to a man. The man disappeared from sight, and the captain returned his attention to us.

"This is an odd gathering," he said.

"How so?"

"All male guests for a household of females." His gaze landed on me. "When did you return?"

"She returned when the home she was at suffered the same searches as our own. There was no point in keeping her away any longer."

His gaze swept over the men.

"Why are you here, Mr. Steinman?"

The man scowled.

"The King pushes too far with these intrusions. I'm here on business, as is every man at this table."

"What kind of business?"

"Trade of course. We have the contacts but lack the funding to move any merchandise."

"And, I have the funding but lack the contacts. It would seem some men think women are only good for marriage and childbirth and do not care to work with a woman in a business sense. These men are more open minded."

The guard the captain had sent away returned with a woman. She was dressed like a maid but wore the King's insignia on her bodice.

"I ask that you step into the hall, one at a time."

"Why?" Maeve asked, her fingers twitching on the table.

"This search will be more thorough. We need to search your person."

CHAPTER FOURTEEN

WHILE PORCIA AND CECILIA MADE SHOCKED NOISES, I stood.

"I'll go first," I said.

"You will not," Maeve said, grabbing for me.

While I had nothing to hide, I knew well that Maeve, Cecilia, and Porcia did. All three wore their amulets as they always did for these gatherings. Likely Maeve's mind was frantically working to find a way to object to a body search.

I lightly set my hand on top of hers and gave her a concerned look.

"Mama, do not let embarrassment rule your thoughts. I made that mistake and was taken to the dungeon and questioned."

Lifting my gaze to the captain who watched us steadily, I repeated my offer to go first. He motioned for me to proceed. Maeve released me with reluctance that I felt was quite true, and I walked into the hall with the King's woman.

The search was thorough as she patted my skirts and pockets. When she reached under my skirts and ran her hands up and down my legs and even cupped my intimate parts, I flushed scarlet.

"If it helps make this less embarrassing, I'm a midwife," the woman said softly. "This is nothing I haven't seen or touched before."

"Since you're not delivering my child at the moment, it does not help," I said, offering a small smile to take the sting from my words.

She chuckled and stood.

"I need to loosen your bodice and check there as well."

"Of course."

Having another woman swipe her hand between the valley of my breasts and under their curves did not bother me as much as when I'd been stripped in front of Hugh. His detached gaze as he'd hit me, without regard as to where, had been far more intolerable.

When the woman stepped away from me and looked at one of the two men who had stood watch over us, there wasn't a bit of me she hadn't touched.

"I found nothing," she said.

The second man went to the captain as the first man's gaze shifted to me.

"Please wait outside."

As I moved toward the door, Cecilia took my place. I

knew it was her by her impertinent, "Remove your hands from my skirt."

Trying not to smirk, I let myself out and found a man with a torch waiting in the yard by the horses. Hugh stood near him, his arms crossed and a sullen look on his face.

"Were you searched, too?" I asked, joining him.

He cast me a dark look and didn't answer. I was no longer sure how much of the old Hugh still remained.

Slowly, every person from the dining room joined us, Maeve walking out the door last. Her gaze connected with Cecilia first, then me, before turning to the guard.

"Is there a reason we must stand in the cold now that we've been thoroughly violated?" she asked.

"The violation would have been more enjoyable if it had been the maid who'd done the searching," one of the men commented.

Maeve shot the man a scathing look.

"Is that how you truly feel?" she asked.

The man flushed and looked away just as the captain emerged from the kitchen door with the midwife in tow.

"You may return to your dinner," he said. "Again, I apologize for the inconvenience of this search, but I assure you we are making the Kingdom safer through our diligence."

"Are you, though?" I asked.

All eyes turned to me.

"I beg your pardon?" the captain asked.

"Are you making the Kingdom safer? If you're still

searching, wouldn't that mean the problem still exists? Instead of making us feel safer, these searches are spreading fear. One woman in the market today said her family was leaving soon because of the way His Majesty is treating his subjects. If this continues, His Majesty will be a King of a kingdom without a people."

"Twit," Cecilia said under her breath from her place beside me.

"Cow," I said just as softly.

A man behind us snorted a laugh.

"Cecilia and Porcia, go inside," Maeve said before turning to her guests. "Gentleman, I think we should reschedule this meeting for another evening. I fear the meal my help made is now either cold or dry and inedible."

The men dispersed, and the guards moved to watch them climb into their shared carriages, leaving Maeve and me with the captain.

"I heard you were bold with your speech in the dungeon as well," he said, considering me.

"I've earned more than a few slaps in my life for speaking freely."

"I can imagine so," he agreed.

"However, you cannot refute my daughter's logic. The King's searches are not fixing whatever problems are plaguing him," Maeve said, wrapping her arm around me. "If you have no further questions for us, I think it's time I take Eloise inside before she upsets anyone other than her sister."

The captain's lips twitched at that, and he winked at me.

"You're not a twit. Don't let her goad you."

"Yes, sir," I said as if I truly admired him and his wisdom.

Maeve walked me to the house as the guards mounted their horses and rode off. Cecilia opened the door for us. Stepping inside, I heard the light clank of cutlery from the dining room as Catherine and Heather began cleaning the table. I was relieved they had a reprieve for tonight.

"What are we going to do, Mama?" Cecilia asked after a quick glare in my direction.

Maeve released me as she drew in a slow breath.

"It's time to do something to hasten the Prince's return. Cecilia, fetch what we need from the dining room. Porcia, fetch a knife and a bowl."

Maeve had only ever used magic. Why did she need a knife? My stomach twisted with fear as both her daughters hurried off. In the dining room, Cecilia lifted Maeve's chair cushion and removed an amulet.

"You've impressed me a great deal today," Maeve said drawing my attention. "If not for your quick thinking, it would have been me they had searched first."

The mask holding back my frustration and hate almost slipped.

"I'm glad I was of use."

"You're always of use, my precious girl," Maeve said.

"Come with me." She took my hand and led me to the mirror.

"Mirror, mirror, against the wall. Answer now my humble call. The King still plagues me with his power and might. Show me those who are often in his sight."

The mirror's fog lifted and started showing image after image of royal servants, the King's advisors, and other people.

"Go back," Maeve said. "Yes, that one."

It was a man who stood very close to a void. When he spoke, his words sounded as if they were coming from a great distance, an echo that wasn't easy to distinguish or hear.

"Fear is spreading because of the searches, Your Majesty."

A sigh resonated through the mirror.

"Fear is better than more death," a voice said. "Continue with the searches. She must be found."

"Mama?" Porcia said, drawing Maeve's attention from the mirror.

I turned and saw Porcia offering Maeve a kitchen knife. Maeve took the knife, testing its edge before looking up at Cecilia, who was rejoining us along with Heather and Catherine. The pair cowered side by side, their steps reluctant as they trailed behind Cecilia.

When Cecilia stood before Maeve, she placed one of the amulets around her mother's neck then handed Porcia hers.

"Thank you," Maeve said. She looked at Heather and Catherine. "You have served us well. I would ask one more service before I set you free."

"Yes, My Lady," Heather said. Catherine looked too frightened to speak.

"I need a finger from each of you." As she spoke, Cecilia grabbed Catherine's hand and Porcia grabbed Heather's. Maeve sliced the smallest finger from both of them before I could blink. Time seemed to slow in the seconds that followed. The fingers fell. Both maids stared at the bloodless stumps on their hands. Catherine wailed first. Heather moaned and brought her hand to her chest. Blood started pouring from both of them.

"Porcia, you were supposed to catch them with the bowl," Maeve said, her voice laced with warning.

"S-sorry, Mama." Porcia's eyes looked wide in her pale face as she stared at the fingers on the floor.

Maeve lashed out and slapped Porcia hard.

"Say it correctly."

"I'm sorry, Mama," Porcia said, showing no indication she was even aware of the handprint now enflaming her cheek.

Porcia quickly bent to pick up the fingers and place them in the bowl, which she held out before both women. Cecilia pried Heather's hand away from her body and held it over the bowl, letting the blood drip over the fingers. Catherine quickly held her hand out, terror and pain accentuating the whites of her eyes.

"Blood and bone make my wish be known," Maeve said in a clear voice that rang in the hall.

Her amulet began to glow brightly, and she handed Cecilia her knife. With her hands free, Maeve lifted them toward Heather and Catherine, drawing from them the same green she'd drawn from the men.

"Let a sickness quietly grow and spread. Let those in contact fall gravely ill but not dead. To the proclamation bell I bind this curse. Only with the Prince's return will the sickness disperse."

Both women quieted, their eyes shifting to me. I moved to step forward, to intervene in some way, but Porcia gently laid her free hand on my arm. I didn't look at her, but at Cecilia's provoking smile. She wanted me to interrupt. My gaze shifted to Maeve as she moved her hands toward the mirror.

"Now, Porcia," she said.

Porcia gave my arm a quick squeeze then released me to throw the contents of the bowl at the mirror. Blood coated the glass, and I watched the fingers tumble along the surface to the ground. In the mirror, the man next to the void coughed lightly.

"It is done," Maeve said.

A wet gurgling noise erupted behind me at the same time something spattered my back. I whirled just in time to see Catherine fall to the floor and Cecilia's blade swipe across Heather's throat. The blood sprinkled my dress and Maeve's.

"No," I gasped watching Heather clutch her throat. Her gaze held mine as she slowly crumpled.

The anger I'd been holding back for so long exploded within me. Disregarding the danger of the knife still gripped in Cecilia's hands, I flew at her. My fist landed a solid blow before I froze, suspended mid-movement.

"Girls, that's enough," Maeve said calmly. "When I release you, I expect proper behavior."

Cecilia's gaze danced with pure loathing as the magic freed us. I stepped back though I didn't want to. Cecilia's blade flicked out, and a small cut opened on my forearm.

"That's for calling me a cow."

"Cecilia, you can clean up the mess you made."

The victorious smile fell from her face as she looked at Maeve.

"But, Mama—"

"Now."

"Porcia, help Eloise bind that cut."

"Yes, Mama," Porcia said. She took my hand and tugged me from the room, making a wide circle around the bloody pool spreading beneath Catherine and Heather's bodies. Numbly, I followed, blood trailing down my arm and dripping to the floor as we made our way through the dining room to the kitchen.

Food waited on the cutting board, remnants of the meal Heather and Catherine had been clearing away that was a glaring reminder of what had just been lost. I blinked, trying to recall when everything went so terribly wrong.

When the guards had arrived, I'd hoped it would mean our freedom. If I'd known Heather and Catherine would die if I'd stood first...

A tear fell from the corner of my eye.

"Don't," Porcia said in a forceful whisper. She gripped my shoulders and shook me until I focused on her. "Don't ever cry. Do you understand? The weak do not survive."

I blinked, forcing away the pain.

"Do the strong, though?" I asked.

"You're still here, aren't you?"

She released me and fetched some cloth strips that we used for our monthlies. I held out my arm as she washed and bound the wound.

"Why are you here?" I asked. "Why am I still alive?"

She looked up at me, our gazes holding for a long time.

"I'm here because I learned not to be weak. Just like you're learning."

In that moment, I saw a hint of past pain in her eyes.

"You don't want to be Cecilia's enemy," she said. "Find a way to make it right."

Her words, so close to Maeve's, made me frown.

"Perhaps it's Cecilia who doesn't want to make an enemy of me."

Porcia snorted and tied the ends of the bandage.

"Cecilia killed Catherine and Heather like she did because she knew it would hurt you. Would you have done the same to hurt her?"

HAUNTED BY THE DEATHS, I slept very little; so, with the first light, I rose and went outside to wash the blood from my dress. It took a long while to work the stains free, but I didn't mind. I thought of Catherine and Heather. Of the little ways they'd helped me. How, in the end, I'd been unable to do the same.

While Porcia's thinking would see the blame of their deaths on my shoulders, I knew where it belonged. I hated Cecilia almost as much as I hated Maeve, now. But my hatred and anger would need to remain hidden for a time yet.

When the dress was clean, I hung it out and went inside. The house was still quiet. I found some bread and cheese, which I sliced. I ate half and made up a plate with the rest. Leaving the kitchen with the plate in hand, I went up to Maeve's room and knocked softly on the door.

"Who is it?" she called softly.

"Eloise, Mama."

"Come in."

I opened the door, entering her room for the first time since I fled it weeks ago. Maeve was sitting up in bed, looking at me with curiosity.

"What's wrong?" she asked.

"Nothing. I brought this for you, thinking no one else would." I moved closer to the bed, sitting on the edge like I would have done for my own mother, and handed her the plate.

"Thank you," she said. "But you know this work is beneath you."

"You, as well."

She smiled and lifted a hand to smooth over my hair.

"Would it be all right with you if I went to the market early?" I asked. "This is the best time of day to watch and listen for news of the sickness."

She beamed at me.

"Very clever of you. Yes. You should wake Cecilia so she can go with you."

"Why does she hate me?" I asked boldly.

Maeve picked up a slice of cheese, studying it thoughtfully before looking at me.

"That's often the way between sisters. They compete for their mother's affection or the most handsome man in the kingdom."

"I'm not trying to steal affection or a man, though."

Maeve chuckled and patted my cheek.

"Go. Get your information. Tell Cecilia that she and Porcia should make the rounds, too. You might want to wake Porcia first."

She settled against her pillows, and I knew I was dismissed.

Leaving her room, I went to Porcia's room first, like Maeve had advised, and knocked on her door. She opened it, looking tired and decidedly annoyed.

"Mama wants us to go to town now for news," I said. "Cecilia is supposed to come with us, too."

"I do not envy you waking her," Porcia said. "I'll be ready shortly." She closed the door in my face.

Turning, I went to Cecilia's door, knocked loudly, and stepped back. When the door flew open, I was ready for her scowl.

"Mother wants us to leave for town immediately," I said.

Her eyes narrowed.

"Mother would never wake me this early."

I lifted my hand and gestured to Maeve's closed door down the hall.

"Go ask her if you must. I'll wake Hugh and be waiting for both you and Porcia outside."

I turned and was about to walk away when she grabbed my hair and pulled me back. I didn't cry out or struggle. Instead, I tilted my head as much as I was able and looked at her.

"I wanted to go alone. She insisted you go, too. I'm to walk the market and you're to make social calls with Porcia."

A smug smile curved her lips, and she released me with a shove. She didn't see my answering smile as I descended the stairs. As Porcia said, I was learning. I had no choice. I either played their game or died like Catherine and Heather. It was time to move beyond manipulation and subtle defiance. It was time to show them all how strong I could be. I would be risking everything, but I saw no other way.

Hugh grumbled about the hour but quickly readied the carriage when I said it was Maeve's wish we leave immediately. The ride to town was tense and quiet. Hugh dropped me off in the market district then took Cecilia and Porcia away.

I walked along the market, speaking with a person here and there, watching for signs of sickness. There weren't any, for which I was grateful. If there had been, I would have had no reason to leave the market.

Keeping a friendly smile on my face, I started on the route that would either lead to my salvation or demise.

I walked toward the Brazen Belle.

CHAPTER FIFTEEN

A HUSH BLANKETED THE WHOREHOUSE THIS MORNING. A FEW patrons snored on the porch, likely the same place where they'd fallen asleep in a drunken stupor the night before.

Without hesitation, I walked boldly up the front steps and entered the establishment's large common room. It was less debasing than the back room I had been in previously. The women were covered, mostly, and there were tables and a bar for food and drink.

One of the serving women, sitting at a table, looked up at me, boredom in her gaze.

"Your nilly need a lick?" she asked. "I can do it for three coppers."

I had no idea what she meant by nilly but knew I didn't want her licking anything of mine.

"No, thank you. I'm here for Rose."

"She's in the kitchen. Sleeps by the fire." She waved me

off and resumed her bored picking of loose stitches on her gaping bodice.

Leaving the common room for the direction she'd waved, I stepped into the kitchen. Rose lay on a mat near the dying fire. As I watched, she shivered lightly in her sleep. Despite knowing what she was, I went to place more wood on the fire for her.

"That's kind of you," she said softly without opening her eyes. "Kindness is not often freely given."

"I used to think it was," I said, sitting on the stool near her so we could continue to speak quietly.

She opened her eyes to look at me.

"I thought you might be back. Too bad talking to the tree didn't work."

"How did you know?"

"A little bird told me," she said with a wry smile.

"I need your help."

She chuckled.

"I knew that when you first tried to speak and couldn't. But I can't help you. That curse holding your tongue is layered and deep. Only the one who cast it can remove it before it's done."

"Done?"

"All curses have an end. Once the goal is met, the curse will break on its own."

I thought of the curse that Maeve cast last night. How the ill would become well again once the bells tolled to announce the Prince's return.

"I don't want you to remove it. I want something else. What I want will likely place you in grave danger, though. You might already be in danger, now, just for speaking with me. And, I have no means to compensate you for your help."

The old woman cackled softly.

"You have means of which you do not yet know." She motioned for me to help her up. Her grip was strong on my arm as she struggled to her feet.

"As for the danger," she said, straightening to her full height, which towered a few inches over me, "I've never been bothered by it before. Why should I start today? Tell me what it is you ask of me."

"Can you cast a spell on me to prevent any physical injury?"

She gazed at me thoughtfully.

"Is someone hurting you?"

"I can't answer that."

She studied me a moment then frowned.

"You already have a layer of protection."

"How do you explain the bruises?"

"This protection is something deeper. An awareness of others. A sense of danger."

I snorted.

"Well that failed me, too, when the—" I wanted to scream.

Rose gave me a pitying look. "I can give you something more. Something that will reflect any physical blow."

"Not reflect. Absorb."

"Are you certain you don't want to see the one hurting you hurt in return?"

I looked at the floor, trying to think of something to say to help her understand. "If you and I were in a field together, and I struck a bull with a sword then hid, would the bull look for me because I struck it or would it attack you because you were there at the time it was angered?"

"Ah. You're protecting someone else. Won't this person be hurt in your place?"

I thought of Kellen's peaceful face the last time I saw her and hoped not. Yet, I could no longer keep choosing her life over others. The memory of how it felt when the droplets of Catherine's blood hit my back would haunt me forever, and I didn't want more of such memories.

"Perhaps. But it's a risk I must take. And after you cast the spell, I'll need you to cast another."

Rose's brows rose.

"Another? You ask much."

"Once you're finished, I cannot be allowed to speak of what you've done for me. For your protection and for those I protect."

She studied me intently.

"That I can do."

"Will casting these spells hurt anyone?"

Her expression softened.

"No, child. No one will be harmed. Are you ready?"

She held out her hand to me. I glanced down at it, hesitating to put my trust in the woman before me.

"What did he do?" I asked, meeting her gaze.

"Pardon?"

"The pig. What did he do to cause you to curse him?"

She laughed slightly.

"You are a clever girl."

"I've been hearing that a lot lately."

She grinned and took my hand. A tingle of energy swept through me.

"The creature you care for wasn't always a pig. I only gave him his true form. Helped him, if you will."

The tingle grew stronger, burning its way under my skin to my very bones. I gasped then cried out. She placed her hand over my mouth to muffle the sound.

"Just a bit more," she said. "You're doing well."

The heat intensified until it felt like fire in my blood. Darkness swamped my peripheral; but before I welcomed its embrace, the heat vanished, replaced by a cooling numbness.

"There you are," she said, removing her hold. "By word and deed, you will not break or bleed. Nothing made of magic or by man will harm you. You will not speak of this or any past dealings with me, save in reference to the old woman whose pig you still tend. Both spells will break the moment you wed."

"Wed? Why then?"

"Because you won't need the protection of the spell when you have the protection of a husband."

"What if it's a prospective groom who is beating me?"

She patted my cheek.

"You're too clever to marry a brute. Trust me. You will not need it once you wed."

"How do you get your power if not by taking life?"

Rose's brows lifted.

"You are in a dangerous position, aren't you? How are you here?"

"Obedience won me some limited freedom. But I'm never truly free. What's been done here might already be known."

Rose cackled.

"That's very unlikely, child. This is my domain. What happens here is always private."

I stood, hoping she was right.

"Thank you for your help."

"You're welcome. As for your payment, I will call upon you in the future should I have a need of something. No more than two small favors. In addition to what I've already given you, I will tell you this. Magic is nothing more than the manipulation of the power in every living thing around us. To most it's an intangible energy. To a few gifted, it's the means to rule the world or to help those they love most."

I nodded, not entirely certain I understood what she meant. She seemed to sense that because she grinned at me and waved me off.

"Go. You'll want to set that clever mind of yours on a reason why you visited a whorehouse."

"I already have one. Has anyone gotten ill here?"

The humor left Rose's eyes.

"Two girls last night. Why?"

I shook my head and shrugged. "Do you know who they had entertained?"

"A guard from the castle, I believe."

I nodded.

"Thank you, Rose."

She didn't stop me from walking out. There were a few more patrons in the common room. One of the girls coughed lightly as she spoke to a man more interested in her breasts than her health. I hurried out the door.

The warmth of the day wrapped around me as I made my way back to the market. Vendors were set up now and fully shouting the superiority of their goods. I stopped at a stall to purchase something to eat and saw the vendor cough lightly. Moving on without ordering, I saw more signs of sickness already spreading in the market.

My stomach growled, and I wondered if Rose's spell would protect me from falling ill. Another thought struck me, and I couldn't help but smile at the thought of Cecilia being struck by this magical plague. Nothing would give me more pleasure than to see her suffer. Well, perhaps nothing other than Maeve's own suffering.

Not far from me, a woman coughed into her apron and

the material came away bloody. The person she was speaking to saw the stain and backed away. A nearby vendor coughed, the sound wet and gurgling and looked at his hand.

"Sickness," someone said.

A hush consumed the immediate area before everyone started yelling and moving. Some fled the market, likely for fear of becoming ill. Others remained, looking lost as they too began to cough.

"The King will help us, right Mama?" a child asked his sick mother.

"Yes, darling. He will."

Despite the recent searches that had scared so many, our ruler was still well loved. I wondered how long that would continue as the sickness Maeve had created slowly brought the Kingdom to its knees.

I left the market and waited near the spot where Hugh and the sisters had left me. It didn't take them long to return. Hugh coughed lightly into his hand after he pulled the carriage to a stop.

"I'll open the door for myself," I said quickly.

When I climbed in, Cecilia and Porcia were sitting opposite one another. I took the seat beside Porcia, and she gave an aggrieved sigh.

"You should have ridden on top with Hugh," Cecilia said, a knowing smile on her face.

"How many people have fallen ill?" I asked.

"Not many," Cecilia said with a shrug. "But it doesn't

matter. There is no doubt that mother's spell will work. It's only a matter of time before the King falls ill."

Her smugness ate at me. I wanted to strike out at her. Knowing that there would be no repercussions only made the urge harder to resist. Yet, I did resist it. If Maeve did not yet know what I'd done, I would prefer to keep it secret as long as possible, for I now had a plan.

MAEVE WAS PACING the steps when we pulled into the yard. Through the window of the carriage, our gazes locked. The rage there didn't bode well for me. But, I didn't regret my decision, and I hoped my feelings would remain unchanged no matter how she sought to punish me for what I'd done.

"Where were you?" she demanded when I stepped down. "You were in the market, and then you were gone. The mirror would show me nothing." Her gaze flicked from me to Hugh, and I lifted my hands, pleadingly as I sidestepped his meaty fist.

"I went to the Brazen Belle, Mama. Please."

She motioned for Hugh to stay.

"Explain yourself. Why did you leave the market?"

"The market was quiet, which I would expect at the hour, and I saw no one ill. Since the sickness started with a man in the castle, a man close to the King and to the guards, I went to the place the guards would most likely go during their free time to determine if the sickness was spreading. I didn't know the mirror wouldn't be able to find me. I swear. And, I did find sickness at the Brazen Belle. Two of the girls were already abed with it, and another coughed in the common room as she spoke to one of the men. When I returned to the market from there, I saw signs of it in the increased crowd. It's spreading quickly, and people are beginning to panic." I gestured to Hugh. "Hugh's coughing, too."

A slow smile curled Maeve's lips.

"Very well done, Eloise, my sweet. I apologize for getting so angry for nothing."

Cecilia made a small noise. When I glanced her way, she was glaring at me. Beside her, Porcia had gone pale and watched her sister with a hint of dread.

Maeve reclaimed my attention by wrapping her arm around my shoulder and hugging me to her side.

"What kind of reward would you like?" she asked.

"Reward?" The word struck fear in me. Maeve's rewards were often a calm before a new storm.

"I need no reward, Mama. Helping is enough."

"Come, now," she squeezed my arm harder. "I insist."

I glanced at Cecilia and Porcia. The hate in Cecilia's eyes only burned brighter now.

"I don't want any of us to fall ill," I said, looking up at Maeve. "Cecilia and Porcia are my sisters. I would spare them from what I saw. Coughing up blood cannot be pleasant. Hugh too, if it's possible."

"Consider it done."

I glanced at Cecilia, but her expression hadn't changed. If she tried hurting me again, my secret would be discovered far too quickly.

"You three go inside and fix us something to eat. I'll see if I can do something to make Hugh feel better."

The purr that had crawled into her voice made me sicken. I could well imagine what she intended to do with Hugh. I only hoped he would be cured of the plague in the process.

Following a healthy distance behind Porcia and Cecilia, we made our way to the kitchen door. As soon as it closed behind us, Cecilia whirled on me.

"You simple fool," she snarled. "You wasted a gift rarely given on an unnecessary request."

"I don't understand," I said. "I was trying to make amends."

"Amends?" She growled and paced the room. "We are her daughters. We are essential to Mama's plans. Of course she wouldn't allow us to fall ill. Not this close to the Prince's return. You could have had anything. You could have asked her to bring your sister home or to set her free, and Mama would have done it." Cecilia rounded on me. "She will never give you this opportunity again."

I didn't let her words distract me from the moment.

"I understand that you want to blame me, but know that my ignorance is not my fault. You both know Mama and her ways better than I. Either of you could have spoken to me. Could have helped me understand. As I said, I was trying to make amends. I want the anger between us gone."

Cecilia stared at me for a long moment.

"So long as she treats you like her favorite, that will never be."

I sighed.

"I don't seek her favor; you know that. Your anger is misguided."

"Are you suggesting I should be angry with Mama?"

"I suggest nothing. I'm only stating the truth."

She cast a glare at me then looked at Porcia.

"I have a headache. You can help Eloise make us something to eat. I'll be upstairs."

Porcia said nothing as Cecilia stormed from the room. But the look she gave me afterward was just as full of anger as Cecilia's.

"How have I angered you?" I asked, pretending to be exasperated.

"You are far from ignorant. Mother's proclaimed your cleverness time and again. Surely you knew she wouldn't allow us to fall ill. You purposely chose no reward."

"Untrue. Mama's," I said, stressing the word since she'd used the word mother, "lessons can be quite severe. I wasn't at all certain we wouldn't fall ill."

Some of the anger left Porcia's eyes.

"Go fix lunch," she said, sitting at the table.

Uncaring that she wasn't willing to help, I began fetching what I needed to make a light soup. However, the distant clanging of bells reached my ears before I managed to cut more than one slice of bread. I looked at Porcia. Her gaze flicked to me then the door.

"Her time has come again," she said softly. "She will finally realize her dream."

I saw the way Porcia's hand trembled.

"What is her dream?"

"To rule," she said simply.

The door banged open and Maeve strode in, her bodice loosely laced. She beamed at both of us.

"The bells have rung for the King's fall from health. The end has begun. Go get Cecilia."

Porcia hurriedly left the kitchen, and Maeve focused on me.

"There is much we need to do now that the time is here." She paced the length of the room, her mind racing. "Your sisters and I will need to gather more power but not here. It's too dangerous with the searches," she said absently. "We'll need to go to the homes. A little from each person as we exchange pleasantries. No more deaths to frighten the King into action. That phase is past us now." She looked at me and smiled again. "Our time is finally here."

"Yes, Mama," I said smiling in return although I had no idea what she was talking about.

"Will you be all right here on your own? While we're in town, I will look for new maids. It wouldn't do to be without help for long."

"I'll be fine. And don't rush selecting the maids. Heather and Catherine were adequate, but if we're to entertain in the same sphere as the King, we'll need help that's more elevated."

Maeve paused her pacing to stare at me.

"Precisely. I had worried over what type of daughter you would be to me. Defiant? Bold? Meek? Loyal? What you are is so much more than a convenient key." She walked to me and hugged me.

"Thank you, Mama," I said, hugging her in return while imagining taking the bread knife and stabbing it into her back.

Cecilia and Porcia entered just then.

Maeve pulled away from me with a knowing smile on her lips and pressed a kiss to my cheek.

"We will return by dinner."

Cecilia glared at me before following her mother out the door. I waited there with the knife gripped tightly in my hand until I heard the carriage leave. As soon as the sound faded, I dropped the knife and checked the window. I was alone. Finally.

Picking up the poker, I went to the entry and gave the mirror a few experimental jabs and hits. Like Maeve's efforts with the rod, the poker did nothing. Scowling, I returned it to its place then went out to the shed. Every tool within the confines of that building failed to make even a mark on the mirror.

I looked around the kitchen but saw nothing useful.

Why couldn't something bash the mirror as easily as I'd bashed Kaven's head? I grinned at the thought, not because it hurt him but because of his continued presence in my life despite all of the things I'd done to him. Kaven was much like the mirror.

Defeated for the moment, I left the house to put away all of the tools, then made my way to my mother's grave. I no longer needed a cloak for the walk as spring had finally obtained its hold over the land from winter's heavy hand. Breathing in the freshness, I wandered the trees until I spotted the clearing again. Birds sang out in welcome, their melodies echoing loudly in the branches. I watched the trees as I sat, waiting. It didn't take long for me to spot Kaven. When I did, I couldn't help my small smile or the heat that burst in my middle when he smiled in return.

"I was ready to knock on your door," he said. Although I knew his words were a tease, they struck fear in me.

"Never do that," I said. "Promise me."

"Are you ashamed of my lowly position?" he asked sincerely, no hurt in his tone.

"You're sitting. Hardly a low position. You could get much lower."

His eyes widened slightly, and his face flushed. I frowned, unsure how my teasing had offended him.

"I only meant—"

He placed a finger over my mouth.

"No, let me keep the image I have. It's a nice one."

My frown deepened, and he chuckled.

"You confuse me, too," he said. "An enticing combination of charm, innocence, and...something more."

"More?"

His gaze dipped to my lips, and I felt my face flush at his meaning.

"You aren't interested in that," I said.

"Untrue. I asked for your patience."

I snorted.

"It's irony that women have the reputation for not knowing their minds when you're the one being unclear."

He gave me a wry smile.

"I cannot argue your sentiment. But I want you to know I'm very interested in you as a woman, Eloise. However, I'm unable to act on it because of my current obligations."

I frowned at him, growing serious.

"What exactly are you asking me to be patient for? Your obligations to serve the Royal family to end? You've waited here alone for weeks now. Summer is nearly upon us. Are you saying that you're about to leave your service to the Crown after all that time? We both know you won't. If it were an option for you, you would have left long ago."

"Maybe there was something else keeping me here."

I looked away from him, studying the blossoms on the tree as reality set in. I could not encourage his interest. Yet, I couldn't do what was necessary to push him away. I liked Kaven, and I hoped that one day, when I clawed my way free of the tangled web of disaster that clung to my life, Kaven would still be there. Waiting for me.

"You have my patience if you give me yours," I said softly.

When I looked up, our gazes collided.

"You have enchanted me like no other."

My eyes widened.

"Don't say that. Never say that."

He nodded slowly in acknowledgement, his gaze never leaving mine. Slowly, he leaned forward.

"Forgive me, Eloise," he said.

I nodded slightly, barely breathing. He smiled, a soft knowing curve of his lips, just before his mouth settled over mine. The touch was light but sent my heart racing. He moved, imprinting upon me the texture of his skin. I inhaled his scent and lifted my hands to his chest.

He pulled away abruptly, placing distance between us and dislodging my touch but not leaving. We stared at one another.

"A first kiss for you, I believe," he said.

"Yes. Unless we count the one where you bloodied my lip."

He chuckled softly and touched my cheek gently.

"I'm relieved to see you recovered. I had truly worried. If not for..." He sighed. "Believe that I wanted to call on you."

"I believe you. But, please don't call on me. Not until I'm ready. There's so much in my life that I'm trying to survive."

I looked at my mother's grave again, astonished that I'd said so much without the spell choking me.

"I understand," he said. "You need time to grieve. I'll wait."

I said nothing to attempt to correct him. Instead, we sat in silence for several long minutes, and my mind drifted to my current dilemma. How did one break a magic mirror?

"What breaks iron?" I asked abruptly.

"Iron? What iron do you need to break?"

"None, actually. I was only curious."

"A strong blow might break it, depending on its thickness."

"What if one isn't strong? Is there a clever way to break it?"

He thought for a moment. "Changing from extreme heat to extreme cold could fracture it perhaps."

I grinned and stood.

"Why do I get the feeling you're off to break some iron?"

CHAPTER SIXTEEN

I HEAVED AGAIN, SWEATING PROFUSELY FROM THE HEAT AND from my effort to drag the mirror through the kitchen door. The memory of Kaven and Kellen, and what was at stake, spurred me to keep going. The door shut behind me and I paused, leaning the mirror against a support to wipe the sweat from my brow.

The fireplace here was the only one large enough for the mirror. Having stoked the fire as soon as I'd returned, the flames already licked their way up the chimney. I hoped Kaven's idea worked and imagined what I would do once the mirror was broken.

Kellen would be safely beyond Maeve's reach. As much as I wanted to race away and rescue my sister, she would need to wait. Too many lives were at risk to selfishly run from what was happening here. I needed to stay and learn what Maeve planned to do. She needed to be stopped.

Thus, my need for Rose's spell of protection. Once I broke the mirror, Maeve's anger would be immeasurable.

Pulling the mirror once more, I worked it over to the fireplace and stood it on its end against the stone. The skin on my hands reddened being so close, and I wondered how I could manage to get the piece into the flames.

In the end, I positioned the stool before the hearth and set the mirror on it, pushing the cursed object close enough that one end was in the flames while the other end was on the stool. It would make it easier to accomplish what I next needed to achieve, which was removing the mirror.

Hurrying to the cold storage, I wrapped a chunk of last winter's ice in a heavy cloth. My arms strained to lift the huge block, and I briefly considered taking one of smaller size. But I needed the weight and the cold if this was to work.

Once it was in my arms, I held it to my chest and stumbled up the stairs, tripping several times on my skirts. Only a quick lean against the wall saved me from toppling down and likely killing myself.

I was panting heavily when I reached the kitchen. However, the mirror's glass was glowing an angry red, giving me hope. I set the ice on the block and unwrapped it. There was no bite of cold to pierce my hands. The block only felt hard and smooth when I touched it directly. However, when I removed my hand from it, I could feel its chill.

Leaving the ice, I went to the mirror. Instead of turning it like I'd planned, I reached my hand toward the flame. My skin warmed to the point of discomfort, and then I felt nothing. I touched a dancing flame. My flesh didn't burn or blacken. I remained unharmed.

Relieved at the proof of Rose's spell, I pulled the mirror directly from the flames and dropped it to the floor. Hurrying to the ice, I hefted it into my arms.

"Please work," I whispered just before I dropped the block on the glass.

The crash was deafening when the two met. The ice shattered into a thousand sharp shards that flew everywhere. Several hit me but didn't leave a mark. Beneath the crush of ice, the mirror's surface remained perfectly unblemished. I stared in horror for several long moments.

"No!"

I picked up the poker and beat the mirror with a rage comparable to Maeve's own.

That was when the door opened.

In my rage, I hadn't heard the carriage pull into the yard. But, I heard Maeve's angry shout a moment before I flew backward, hit by an invisible fist of air, and crashed into the table and bench. It didn't hurt, but it was disorienting. Lifting myself up slowly, I looked at Maeve, fear clawing at me.

Kellen.

"How dare you," Maeve said with a frightening cold

calm. "I was ready to give you everything. You would have had a kingdom at your fingertips, and this is how you repay me? You try to take from me what is mine?"

"Only as you took from me, Mama," I said, standing, determined not to show what I felt.

Her lips pulled back in a silent snarl, and she bent to pick up the poker I'd dropped.

"I will take far more," she said advancing. She struck out, hitting me across the face. The blow moved me. But it didn't hurt.

I reached up to touch my cheek and check for blood as Maeve's gaze narrowed. She hit my hand, bending my fingers. Nothing gave way or broke.

"Who did this to you?" she demanded.

"I would tell you, Mama, but I've been cursed. I cannot speak of it."

She screeched and grabbed me by the arm, dragging me to the fire.

"You will speak."

She pushed me hard. I stumbled over the stool and fell into the hearth. Flames flared over my skirts, consuming the material. I felt nothing. I stood and shook out my skirt, trying to extinguish the blaze. My efforts only made the flames climb higher, devouring my clothes.

Ignoring it, I looked up at Maeve.

"I cannot speak, and I cannot be physically harmed."

Underneath Maeve's bodice, a light began to glow.

"Very well. As you are so keen on layering more spells

upon your person, I will add another. Eloise Cartwright, you are bound to this estate by birth, by name, and by King's decree. And thus your freedom is bound to me."

I laughed, relieved.

"Do you truly believe I want to leave my home? You are mistaken. It's you who needs to leave. You have brought nothing but pain and misery to this home and this kingdom. But to what purpose? Is it truly for the Crown of Drisdall to sit upon your head? Why would you want a paltry command when you have such a formidable power already? Towdown was brought low with a single spell."

"You want to know why? Because I refuse to accept I have lost."

Disbelief robbed me of words. Had I been wrong? Was this about repeating an already failed attempt to wed into the Royal family?

She looked at Cecilia and Porcia.

"Your sister's dress is ruined. Perhaps you can help her."

Cecilia's hand closed over my arm in an unyielding grip.

"With pleasure, Mama." She viciously ripped what remained of the gown from my body, leaving me nude. I lifted my free arm to cover my breasts and attempted to jerk my other arm free.

"Do you think this makes me cower?" I asked, looking at Maeve. "Tremble with fear? This is nothing more than what's already been done to me."

"You're right."

"Porcia, fetch Hugh."

"He can't hurt me."

"Not physically, but there are so many more ways to be hurt, my child." She smiled and stepped closer, sweeping her hand over my cheek in a loving caress that reminded me far too much of Kaven.

"And I am far from done with hurting you."

She patted my cheek gently then looked at Cecilia. Something cold clamped around my wrist, and I looked down at the shackle in dismay.

"Help me with the mirror," Maeve said.

She and Cecilia righted it and leaned it against the butcher block. I saw myself smudged with soot and ash.

Maeve called to the mirror, asking to speak with Grimm. I hardened myself for what was to come. I'd known it was a risk to attempt to break the mirror and cursed myself for losing my temper and not hearing her return. I frowned, realizing Maeve's return had been too opportune.

"You knew," I said suddenly, recalling how she'd known the mirror was close before it had even arrived.

She glanced back at me, away from the emerging image of Grimm.

"Knew what?"

"That I was attempting to destroy it."

"Of course. From your first blow. However, it took time to finish our business and return home."

She smiled and faced Grimm.

"It's time to bring my daughter home by any means necessary, Grimm."

He nodded to her.

"But I prefer alive," she said.

My heart began to race as I imagined the threat coming for Kellen. I hoped the little men who had defended her previously would continue to do so even against a greater number.

The door to the kitchen opened, and Hugh stepped in, followed by Porcia.

"There you are," Maeve said with a purr. She moved to Hugh's side and slid her hand over the front of his trousers.

"Do you know why I spared him?" she asked, looking at me even as a bulge formed under her exploring hand.

"Not only is he young and virile, he is very well endowed. A delicious combination. It's been wrong of me to keep him to myself." She turned to Hugh. "There's no need to be gentle with her. She can't feel any pain. I wonder what she will feel as you hold her down and thrust into her in every way possible." She turned, a slow smile blooming on her face.

Terror engulfed me. I yanked at the chain, forgetting my worry over modesty as I desperately attempted to slip my hand free.

"Come, my darlings," she said. "This is unsuitable for the eyes of proper young ladies."

Cecilia cast a nasty grin at me. "Pain or not, your

screams will echo in this pathetic excuse for a home, dear sister."

Porcia looked at me, her expression unreadable. "Try to learn this time."

Maeve smiled at her and gave her a motherly pat, which earned Porcia a scowl from Cecilia as they left through the dining room door. In the silence, I heard the rustle of cloth and looked at Hugh.

He tugged his shirt from his trousers, his gaze on my breasts. Covering them with my hands did nothing to snuff the single-minded intent reflected in his eyes.

"Don't do this," I said. "She has you under her spell. This isn't you. You would never hurt me."

He paused, and his gaze lifted to mine. A green light flickered in the depths of his eyes.

"Stop me," he whispered. In that brief moment, I heard the torment in Hugh's voice and saw it in his anguished expression. Then it vanished, and the sick pleasure returned as he reached down to rub himself.

"You'll like this," he said. He tugged his trousers open and moved closer to me. "Have you seen a cock before?"

I swallowed hard and backed up a step, the links of chain clanking with the movement.

"I would prefer never to see one," I said.

I sacrificed the arm covering my breasts to fumble behind me for anything that might help. Hugh reached forward, running a finger through the valley of my breasts.

I shivered against the unwanted touch as my hand closed around something.

My eyes began to water when his palm covered one breast, and I eased my other hand from the apex of my legs.

"I've never had a virgin," he said softly.

My grip tightened on the metal, and I trembled with anguish as his fingers gently touched the hair between my legs.

"I'm begging you, Hugh. Don't make me do this."

This man had been with my family for more than half my life. As a child, I'd looked up to him, seeing him more as an older brother or young uncle than random hired help. He'd teased Kellen and me and watched over us. He'd nurtured our curiosity of the woods when Father was away and Mother too ill to leave the house. He taught me how to track the signs animals left behind.

Most importantly, he'd taught me to respect life.

Tears streaming down my cheeks, I shifted the poker in my hand.

"Forgive me," I whispered before thrusting it into his right eye. He screamed loudly and fumbled backward, grasping the iron rod. He pulled it out with another cry, and I gagged at the gore still stuck to the end.

"Bitch!" he roared, coming at me. He struck me in the face, knocking me aside. I fell near the hearth and grabbed a burning log.

Before I could swing it at him, he grabbed it from my hands with a pained grunt and tossed it aside.

"She gave me a task," he panted. He groped in his pants with his good hand and gripped my arm with the burnt one. His expression twisted with a blend of pleasure and pain. I kicked at him and he backhanded me. My chain rattled with our struggles. He lifted me in his arms then slammed me on the ground. Before I knew it, I was pinned under his weight. I could feel him trying to position himself as he held my free arm.

Everything slowed as I looked up at him. His face was bloody and angry. Underneath the mask, I still saw my friend. I saw him as I wrapped the chain around his neck. I saw him as I rolled and squirmed and beat at him. I saw him as his face reddened, and he gasped for air. And finally, at the end, he saw me.

"El..."

It was an apology, not just for the moment but for everything before what just occurred, too.

His weight slumped against me. Because it was wasted by Maeve's magic, it didn't take me long to be free of his body. I sat beside him and silently cried. I cried for everyone I'd lost and everyone I had yet to lose.

I couldn't be sure how long I sat there before Maeve walked in.

"I told you there were more ways to be hurt. You will learn."

Anger blazed inside of me. Releasing his burned hand, I looked up at her.

"This is what you wanted?"

"Not at all. I wanted an obedient daughter. However, this is the bitter lesson that life must often teach us. We will always want what is just out of our reach."

"That's not a life lesson."

Her lips curved in a small smile.

"You are correct. That's our nature."

"Yours, not mine. I want nothing more than what I had before you came."

"That is because you had everything. Live with nothing for a few days and tell me you still need nothing."

She swept out of the room, leaving me as I was. A short time later, Cecilia and Porcia came and removed Hugh's body.

DIRTY, naked, and hungry, I lay on the cold stone before the unlit hearth. Had I been smart, I would have hidden away Hugh's shirt before he was taken to the woods.

Porcia entered the kitchen from the dining room.

"This is all your fault," she said angrily. "We had servants to do this."

"This" was the terribly menial task of slicing bread and salted meat for their morning meal. I turned my head to watch her, unable to help myself. Even day-old bread was better than no bread. Instead of seeing Porcia cutting bread, I saw the reflection of myself on the floor. I was hardly recognizable.

A ripple of something shimmered across the smoky surface. Had I not been staring at the mirror, I would have never noticed it. I glanced at Porcia who continued to grumble, unaware something had just happened. Not that it mattered because Maeve was very aware. She strode into the kitchen several long moments later.

There was a measured amount of impatience in her stride and expression. For two days, the mirror and the bells had remained silent, and Maeve's temperament had deteriorated by the hour. Porcia, well aware of her mother's mood, ducked her head and worked faster as Maeve approached the mirror.

"I am here. Show me who calls."

The mirror's surface clouded then cleared to reveal Grimm. The man looked delightfully terrible. His dirty, worn clothes hung torn and ragged from his body. Color darkened one eye, and his nose appeared swollen and crooked. Tufts of hair stuck out oddly near patches that seemed a bit thin.

"My Lady," he said with a deep bow and reverence.

"Where is she?" Maeve demanded.

"She remains with the small men. Magic protects them all. We could not get to her. I am all that remains. I wanted to gaze upon you one last time before I attempt to retrieve her again."

Maeve made a sound of impatience.

"Stay as you are and wait for my summons."

The mirror dimmed, and I saw Maeve's angry

expression. Porcia, finished with her task of fixing them something to eat, set the knife aside and quietly carried the plate to the table. She said nothing, but Maeve watched her with a narrowed gaze.

"I'm surrounded by incompetent fools," she said softly before focusing on the mirror again. "How can one child elude so many?"

Her gaze met mine in the cloudy surface, and she slowly turned, a smile growing.

"What a sight you are," she said with a low chuckle. "I'm tempted to leave you just as you are. One of the fairest in the land reduced to the look of a starving street beggar. Prince Greydon certainly won't consider you now, will he?"

Cecilia swept into the room, her eyes dancing merrily.

"Of course, he wouldn't. Covered in soot and desperation, Eloise couldn't catch a man fresh from the docks."

Maeve's gaze locked on her daughter.

"Do you truly believe that?"

Some of Cecilia's humor faded as Maeve turned to the mirror.

"Show me the fairest in the land. Those with the beauty to tempt Prince Greydon's hand."

The surface shifted, growing dark for so long that I thought it was trying to indicate no woman would tempt Prince Greydon. Given his arrogant presence, I wouldn't have been surprised. Then the surface lighted, reflecting me even in my current state.

Cecilia gasped softly, and I fought not to laugh at her outrage. My image faded to be replaced by my sister. She once again slept, but far differently from before. She wore a light shift that left nothing to the imagination. Her hair lay in a dark halo around her pale face. Her slightly parted lips and the flush coloring of her cheeks made her seem more woman than young maid. I blinked at my twin in surprise before her image disappeared, and several others flashed on the surface before it finally showed Cecilia and Porcia.

"It will take more than dirt and questionable attire to hide your sister's beauty," Maeve said. There was no anger in her tone, only calculation. I wished I could hear her thoughts.

"Cecilia, go to the market for a piece of fruit. Select the most tempting one you find. Take a horse and make haste. Do not fail me."

"There is bread and meat, Mama," Porcia said softly.

Maeve turned on her youngest.

"The fruit is not for me, my sweet. It is for your sister, Kellen."

I fisted my hands and sat up, fighting the urge to shiver.

"What are you going to do?" I demanded.

"If you both refuse to see your value to me as proper young ladies, then it is my duty, as your mother, to help you learn." She turned to Porcia. "Come, my darling. I will need your help to trick your sister. She will return home on her own once I'm done with her."

CHAPTER SEVENTEEN

PORCIA ENTERED THE KITCHEN AND THREW A HOMESPUN, tawny cloak at me.

"Clean yourself with that, and I'll give you something to wear."

I quickly wiped my face, arms, and legs with the cloak. The yellow-brown color became more muted with my filth by the time I finished and tossed it back to her.

She hung the cloak on the corner of the mirror and left again, leaving me with my reflection. Though dirt no longer marred my face, I looked slovenly. Using my fingers, I combed my hair and created a rough braid in its length. It didn't help. How could the mirror possibly think a pompous ass like Prince Greydon would ever fall for me as I was?

I turned my back to the mirror and sat on the stool to wait for Porcia and my promised clothing. However, that wasn't who entered several minutes later. An old woman shuffled into the kitchen, her brown eyes sweeping the room and landing on the cloak.

Feeling an odd itch of awareness tingle its way up my back, I covered my chest.

She chuckled softly to herself, seeming not to notice me, and continued her slow pace across the room. The dress she wore hung from her thin frame and swished around her bare feet while the long, soft wisps of her light grey hair moved against her shoulders. When she reached the mirror, she tugged the cloak free and met my gaze in the glass.

"I've already seen all that you have, my darling. Covering yourself now is hardly worth the effort."

The words sent a chill through me as I stared into the brown eyes that struck a faint chord of familiarity. Other than a hint in the eyes, there was no resemblance between the woman before me and Maeve. However, the way she continued to study me as she settled the cloak around her shoulders left no doubt.

Porcia entered the room, a simple servant's dress in her arms.

Maeve nodded to Porcia, who handed me the dress. They both watched me step into the skirt then Maeve chuckled when I couldn't place my shackled arm into the sleeve. She waved her hand and the shackle fell away.

It felt good to be free of its weight, and I quickly slipped my arm into the dress.

"You may have clothing," Maeve said. "But you may not yet have your freedom."

The shackle immediately rose up and closed over my wrist again.

"Keep her chained unless there's a raid," Maeve said to Porcia.

"Yes, Mama."

Maeve's gaze drifted to the door a moment before we heard the horse's hooves pound into the yard. Cecilia arrived through the kitchen door a moment later. Her cheeks were rosy and her hair windswept. Her beauty was unmistakable.

She offered Maeve the small basket she carried.

"I picked the best and the worst," she said.

Maeve smiled at her daughter and patted her cheek. "Very clever of you."

I didn't miss the side glance that Cecilia gave me at Maeve's praise.

Maeve plucked an apple from the basket and held it up before the mirror. Its red perfection hinted at a juicy sweet treat.

"Such a rare bounty this time of year," Maeve said.

"It cost a small fortune," Cecilia said. "A boat laden with fruit had just docked."

A glow radiated from Maeve's chest as she gazed at the apple.

"With a bite of this fruit so juicy and sweet, a forbidden fate our Kellen will meet." Maeve's grin widened before she turned her back on me and continued the whispered spell.

Cecilia laughed and clasped her hands, her eyes dancing with delight as I strained to hear what Maeve said. I caught a few words. Sleep. Lover's touch. But nothing that would help me understand what curse she was weaving.

The reflection of green light died and Maeve tucked the apple into her basket before turning toward Cecilia.

"Remove the mirror from Eloise's sight while I'm gone. No need to tempt her. I'll return within three days. Hunt for news of the Prince. I expect glad tidings when I return."

Maeve shuffled to the door then paused before opening it.

"Oh, and see if you can break the protection spell."

With that, Maeve left and Cecilia turned to me with an evil smile.

THE GLOW from Cecilia's necklace faded with her final word. Porcia sat on the bench, watching from a safer distance. This wasn't Cecilia's first attempt to break the spell. I'd felt the unnatural tingle of her magic and hoped this endeavor would fail like the ones before.

Cecilia picked up the fire poker, her face twisting into an evil mask of anticipation. I prepared myself. She knew I wouldn't just stand there and take a blow and was counting on a fight. Which was why they'd shortened my chain for the time being, giving me only seven links. It was the chained arm she meant to hit and hoped to break.

She lifted the poker, and I fisted my hand. She struck fast, bringing the metal rod down on my arm as I kicked out at her. My foot grazed her thigh as the metal touched down on my arm. Light flared where the rod touched my skin, and I watched Cecilia fly across the room with an immense sense of satisfaction. Although I'd told Rose not to reflect back the damage meant for me, that seemed to have changed with Cecilia's last spell.

Porcia's eyes rounded as Cecilia crashed into the cutting block and crumpled to the floor.

"Foolish girl," Porcia said to me before rushing to her sister's side.

"Did it work?" Cecilia asked, her words slurred.

"No. The protection spell's hold seems to have tightened."

She helped Cecilia to her feet.

"Come, sister. Let us rest for a bit then go to town. We must have news before Mama returns."

Cecilia nodded, and I breathed a sigh of relief as the pair finally left me in peace. They had spent a day and a half attempting to break the spell protecting me. Cecilia had even gone so far as to wait until I slept and then attempted to beat me. Although I was unhurt, I was exhausted.

I sat on the stool and stared at the fire's dying embers. Now that I had clothes, there was no reason to withhold heat. Not that having either had greatly improved my situation. Though I was warm, I was still hungry and thirsty. Looking at the table set with bread, cheese, and a pitcher of wine, my stomach growled. Since Maeve left, Cecilia had made sure to leave both food and water visible but out of my reach.

Angry, I turned away from the sight and considered my circumstance and Kellen's. If the little men protecting her had beaten the trackers, perhaps they would see Maeve for what she was and continue to protect my sister. If Maeve failed, that meant she would return here and continue her plan, whatever that may be. And her greatest asset continued to be her damnable mirror and the amulet. Attached to Maeve as it was, the amulet would be as impossible to destroy as the mirror.

Something popped in the hearth, sending embers floating upward. Idly turning the cuff circling my wrist, I tracked the path of one. Like me, it drifted on a course in which it had no control.

I sat there for a long while before I heard the sisters leave through the main door. Bitterly, I hoped Cecilia's ears would ring for a week.

My gaze once more returned to the table. Standing, I grabbed the stool and threw it at the broom propped against the wall. The rod fell sideways, just as far out of my reach as it had been before. Annoyed, I picked up the poker and once more attempted to stretch far enough to catch the longer object, not that the broom would do me much good if I managed to get it. The table was twice its distance from me. But I was tired of doing nothing.

The metal bit into my skin for only a moment before the discomfort vanished. I tugged, and I strained, my anger growing as the end of the poker came within an inch of the broom. I shouted and heaved with all of my might.

Suddenly, I fell forward.

I crashed against the floor in a heap and looked back at the hearth, confused. The chain hung from its anchor, and the manacle lay on the floor, still locked. I lifted my hand, looking at the undamaged skin with a growing smile.

I'd pulled myself free. I stood and rushed for the table only to stop short at the last second. If I ate the food, they would know I could free myself. I would have more freedom if they thought me still contained. Changing course, I went down to the cold storage and found some wilted carrots from last fall. I took three then returned to the kitchen and went to drink my fill from the well.

Breathing deeply, I debated what to do next. They had only just left, and the sun beckoned me to stay in its warmth as long as possible. Giving in to the urge, I walked around the house, following the path to Mother's grave. The birds sang loudly in greeting, and I smiled and twirled, lifting my arms to the sunlight.

Freedom had never felt so fine.

Smiling to myself, I entered the clearing. Instead of sitting on the bench, I walked among the flowers and inhaled their fresh scent until I stood near the tree. The little bird chirped at me in greeting.

"Hello, my little friend. Will you sing me a song?"

It warbled out a few happy notes, and I closed my eyes in contentment for a moment before resuming my circling walk in the flowers. It didn't take long for Kaven to appear. I stopped my wandering steps and watched his approach.

"You look tired," I said.

"So do you and many of the people of Towdown," he said.

I nodded sadly.

"I heard the bells and saw for myself the sickness spreading in the market two days ago."

He moved to the bench and sat, looking up at me.

"I was worried I would need to leave before I saw you again," he said.

"Leave?"

"Yes. With the King ill, the Prince will be expected to return to the castle now."

"Ah." I hadn't considered that and was as relieved that Kaven would be leaving as I was sad. He was the only friend I had left to me.

I sat beside him and leaned my head on his shoulder as I listened to the bird's song.

"I will come back," he said softly, his arm moving around my back.

"No," I said. "After the King is well again and when the

Prince has less need of you, I will come to you. When I'm ready."

He held me close, his fingers tracing patterns on my side before he chuckled.

"Why is it you favor these dresses so?"

I turned my head to look up at him.

"Why ruin perfectly good dresses when I wander the woods?"

"You used to wear perfectly good dresses while climbing through windows."

I grinned.

"And I ruined them."

"Ah. So you're up to no good today?"

"Most definitely."

His laugh ended with a light cough. I jerked my head from his shoulder and looked at him.

"I'll be fine," he said softly.

"We both will," I said before closing the distance between us. At the last moment, he tried to pull back, but I threaded my fingers in his hair and tugged him forward.

Our lips met, and Kaven groaned. The hand at my side pressed into my ribs, pulling me closer and sending waves of warmth and desire through me. I lifted my free hand to his shoulder, exploring the feel of him under his rough coat. He was broad and strong and lifted me into his lap. I settled with a sigh, leaning into him.

His lips brushed mine once more before his tongue swiped my lower lip. I gasped at the sensation and the way it made my heart race. I opened my mouth to him, giving him entrance and trembling at the feel of his tongue stroking mine.

When he pulled back, I was panting for air.

"Eloise, I will come for you," he said firmly, hugging me close and breaking my heart for what could not be.

He didn't stay long after that but left with a resolved set to his shoulders. In the silence that followed, I looked at the bird.

"Why must I lose everyone I love?" I asked softly.

The bird chirped once, a sad note.

"It does not matter whether my motivation is a selfish desire for what I cannot have or the selfless need to save others. This needs to end. I only wish I had the means to break that damned mirror."

Something heavy and dark fell from the tree with a thump. Frowning, I stood and went to investigate. A black rock flecked with shining silver bits lay on the ground. It was no bigger than my hand. I looked up at the tree and watched several blossoms drift to the ground. The bird chirped at me from its branches as if encouraging me to take the rock.

I bent to retrieve it, the jagged edges biting into my palm as I picked it up. The pain did not fade, and I smiled in understanding.

"Thank you," I breathed before running from the clearing.

In the house, I searched everywhere for the mirror

until only one place remained. Maeve's locked room. I grinned and ran to the attic, crawling into the hidey hole that Kellen had discovered. Rummaging through Mother's trunk, I found the second key to Mother's old room. I couldn't stop shaking as I rushed back downstairs and unlocked the door.

Hope fueled me, and resolve anchored me as I stepped into the room and found the mirror near the window.

I smiled at my reflection and lifted the rock. Then, I hesitated. If I did this, then what? I considered several outcomes. The mirror wouldn't break, and I would need to figure out how to slip back into the shackle. Although Maeve would know something had happened, being chained should protect me.

And if the mirror broke? My smile faded, and anger consumed me. I threw the rock. Time slowed. Sunlight glinted off the silver specks as it tumbled through the air. I held my breath, watching its reflection grow larger. The mirror sparked green a moment before the rock connected. Glass shattered outward along with the rock. The green light flared, and the large shards exploded into dust as the rock hit the floor and rolled to my feet.

I watched the black granules rain down on everything near the now empty wooden frame. The wood cracked and curled back in places. In the vacant space that once held the glass, the air shimmered, and the imprint of a face emerged, screaming in rage. It quickly disappeared.

Maeve knew her mirror was broken.

Smiling, I bent to pick up the stone. After locking the door and returning the key, I made my way to the kitchen where I held the stone for a moment, uncertain what to do with it. It seemed only right that, if it had come from Mother, I returned it to her.

Light played on its surface as I left the house and walked the path to the clearing. Digging a small hole in the earth above Mother's grave, I hid the one object that could hurt me through the protective spell.

"It worked," I said, patting the soil. "But I cannot yet leave, not until I know everything. I cannot allow more people to suffer as we have."

I returned to the house, drank my fill of water, then used some grease to slide my hand back into the shackle. Content, I put more wood on the fire and sat on the stool to wait.

The light faded from the sky before Porcia and Cecilia returned. I heard their laughter and animated conversation in the yard as they unsaddled the horse and approached the house.

"It won't be long now," Cecilia was saying as she opened the door.

Her gaze fell on me, and her smile widened.

"We have glorious news, sister. Mama will be so pleased when she returns."

I couldn't help the small smile that curved my lips.

Nothing would assuage Maeve's anger when she returned.

CHAPTER EIGHTEEN

CECILIA TIPPED HER HEAD TO LOOK AT ME.

"You don't believe me?"

"I do," I said smoothly. "And I hope that the news, whatever it may be, will please Mama enough that I might have a bit of food and something to drink."

Cecilia's smile grew beatific. She crossed the room, took a piece of bread from the plate, and threw it to me. I greedily grabbed it from the air and shoved it in my mouth. My stomach growled ravenously as I chewed.

"The news has pleased me enough that I will give you a bite to eat," Cecilia said.

I swallowed.

"What is the news?" I asked, already knowing what she would say.

"The Prince is returning soon," Porcia said with barely contained excitement, earning a glare from Cecilia.

"Why hasn't the bell tolled?" I asked.

"Because he's not yet here," Cecilia said. "But he will be based on the proclamations we saw all over town. In less than three days, there will be a ball. The first of many. For the next month, the kingdom will celebrate the Prince's return in grand style and welcome."

It made no sense to me. Why would they post about balls and celebration when so many were ill and suffering? Did the Royal family truly not care about their people?

Cecilia reached into her bodice and withdrew a square of parchment.

"They are playing right into our hands," she said, offering it to me.

I unfolded the proclamation and read the slanted script with care.

LET IT BE KNOWN,

To celebrate Prince Greydon's return in three days hence, the first in a month-long succession of grand balls will be held at sunset at the palace. Invitations will be delivered to all families in good standing with the Crown. Those who do not receive an invitation are invited to join the festivities outside of the palace gates. All are welcome to joyously greet our kingdom's most adored son.

.   .   .

I ALMOST ROLLED my eyes but managed to continue reading.

IN A MONTH HENCE, Prince Greydon will select his next bride or the Crown will fall to his successor. The bride must be of virtue and willingly submit to trials by magic to ensure there are no illusions to hide age or disadvantage. The Prince will wed a fair maid of his own age or forfeit his crown.

King Aftan

I READ the last paragraph twice more. Maeve had the power and skill to change her appearance to look of an age to the Prince. But it seemed that the King was anticipating that.

"How will this make Mama happy?" I asked, looking up. "She will be discovered during the trials, won't she?"

Cecilia laughed, nearly dancing back to the table to throw me another piece of bread. I willingly ate it and waited for her to explain. I knew she wouldn't pass an opportunity to show me how unclever I really was in her eyes.

"Do you really think Mama brought us here so she could marry the Prince?"

I nearly choked on my bread and looked at Porcia, who watched me with a small smile.

"Isn't it obvious to you yet?" Cecilia asked. "The King's

health is questionable, and Prince Greydon is coming home to wed and produce an heir. The ball will be the event of the century. Every eligible maiden of good breeding will attend."

"In good standing with the Crown," I said, quoting the proclamation.

"And who is in better standing than the daughters of the woman who saved the kingdom? One both fair and dark as night. The other golden and kissed by the sun."

Cold understanding bloomed. Not only had my mother died so Maeve could position herself and her daughters close to the Royal Retreat, but so Maeve could use the identities of Margaret Cartwright's daughters to gain an invitation to a ball Maeve had ensured would happen. A ball where the Prince would select his future wife.

"Prince Greydon will take one look at me and fall madly in love," Cecilia said. "I hear his late wife and I share many similarities."

I recalled the words I had overheard long ago about this estate being the gateway to the Crown for them. They didn't mean to kill the Royal family, they meant to become part of it. What better way to overthrow the ruler? It would be subtle, and I had no doubt that the King and Prince would likely both mysteriously fall ill as soon as the new wife became pregnant.

"If you're meant to marry Prince Greydon, why am I still alive?"

Some of Cecilia's humor faded.

"Not only are you and Kellen the daughters of Margaret Cartwright, you're also the fairest in the land without need of spells or powders."

Maeve's question to the mirror about the fairest in the land made more sense. They'd known before ever coming here who might distract the Prince from Cecilia's beauty.

"The more reason to—" The words stopped, but there was no painful squeeze.

"Mama had hoped that she could bend to her will the fairest in the land, the true daughters of Margaret Cartwright. It would have made success that much sweeter knowing she'd bested the woman who'd bested her."

"Bested her? I don't understand."

"Don't you? It was Mama who tried to take the kingdom all those years ago. She'd gathered her strength after the King spurned her as his choice for wife and struck hard and fast. It would have worked if not for your mother's clever wit."

Cecilia took the paper from me.

"It was a proclamation much like this one that ruined Mama's chance to be a queen in her own right. But this will help rectify the mistakes of the past. I will wed Prince Greydon, and I will be Queen. Mama will have a kingdom at her fingertips through me."

Disbelief held my tongue. Maeve had been using pawns and appearances for a very long time to keep up her pretense of respectability. Once she was in the palace, I couldn't help but think she would tire of using Cecilia as her mouthpiece.

"And now that Mama doesn't need me anymore?" I asked. "Will I die when she returns?"

"If she wanted you dead, she would have killed you when she arrived. No, she'll want you to bear witness to her greatness and to know that your mother was nothing more than a temporary obstacle easily overcome and forgotten."

She smiled and swept from the room, Porcia following in her wake. As they moved away from the kitchen, they spoke of seamstresses and the gowns they would have made.

Turning toward the dying embers, I smiled and made a vow.

My mother risked her life to protect the kingdom, and I would do no less. Maeve and her daughters could not be allowed the throne. I let the cinder of my anger flame to life.

I knew the name of my mother's murderer, and now I knew why she'd died.

It was time to claim my revenge.

THANK YOU FOR READING DISDAIN! The Tales of Cinder will conclude with Damnation. Keep reading for a sneak peek!

AUTHOR'S NOTE

Poor Eloise! Her life has changed so drastically since the beginning of book 1. Not surprising, really. I knew when I read the original Cinderella tale that whoever I wrote in as the "wicked stepmother" would need to be bad. I mean really bad. Have you read the original? It's incredibly short, but deeply disturbing in what the stepmother made her own daughters do to win the prince. Maeve's character took on an unpredictable life of her own in my head. Her backstory, which will be lightly mentioned in the next book is just the tip of what made her into who she is.

For those of you in my fan groups, you probably recognized the name Heather. She's an author friend of mine who critique reads for me and volunteered as tribute when I needed names for the maids. Let me tell you, when I wrote book 1, I had NO idea what would happen to the maids in book 2. The other maid was named Amber for my friend and assistant Bam. Because of what their characters ended up having to do and endure, I suggested they pick replacement names. Amber graciously agreed so readers wouldn't think I hated the pair of them. Heather, however, loved the idea of her character and didn't mind her tarnished reputation as a whore. Lol

I can't wait to share the final book in this trilogy with you! So much has happened and so much is yet to come. To be sure you don't miss out on any release news, sign up for my newsletter at mjhaag.melissahaag.com/subscribe or join my fan group the Curvy Cartel on Facebook. Hope to see you there!

Happy reading!

Melissa

CHARACTER LIST

Eloise - *Cinderella* (Twin daughter of Margaret and Atwell).

Kellen - *Snow White* (Twin daughter of Margaret and Atwell).

Margaret Cartwright - Eloise and Kellen's mother.

Atwell Cartwright - Eloise and Kellen's father.

Hugh - A stablehand.

Judith - A housemaid.

Anne - A housemaid

Lady Maeve Grimmoire - Kellen and Eloise's new guardian.

Elspeth - A caster who Margaret knew.

Rose - A caster/enchanter.

Catherine - A housemaid.

Heather - A housemaid.

Aftan - The King of Drisdall

Sevil - The deceased Queen of Drisdall.

Greydon - Prince of Drisdall.

Grimm - A tracker/huntsman.

Cecilia - Maeve's daughter.

Porcia - Maeve's daughter.

Disdain is the second Tale of Cinder, which takes part in the Beastly Tales world. If you haven't yet read the Beastly Tales, you're missing out on a seductively dark Beauty and the Beast retelling. There's character cross over between the two trilogies that you're going to love.

SERIES READING ORDER

Beastly Tales

Depravity

Deceit

Devastation

Tales of Cinder

Disowned (Prequel)

Defiant

Disdain

Damnation

Resurrection Chronicles

(zombies and hottie demons!)

Demon Ember

Demon Flames

Demon Ash

Demon Escape

Demon Deception

Demon Night

More to come!

Connect with the author

Website: MJHaag.melissahaag.com/

Newsletter: MJHaag.melissahaag.com/subscribe

"A rider," Cecilia said.

The thunder of hooves outside abruptly stopped. Porcia rose to see who it might be; but before she crossed half the room, the door flew open.

Maeve stormed into the kitchen, still disguised as the old crone. Her cloudy gaze swept the room, noting her daughters then me. I didn't miss the lingering look she gave the manacle circling my wrist. Just as I didn't miss the extra dirt that now clung to her cloths or the new rips to her garments. Whatever Maeve had done hadn't been easy.

"Mama," Porcia said in shock. "We weren't expecting you for another day."

Maeve lashed out, striking her daughter across the face.

"Do not speak," she said in her deep, grating voice.

Porcia's lifted her hand to hold her cheek then thought better of it and clasped her hands in front of her instead.

Cecilia remained at the table, wisely not speaking as she warily watched her mother. Not that Maeve noticed.

She remained focused on me as a pulse of green light started at her chest. The glow grew larger and brighter with each beat until the emerald radiance enveloped her. The lines on her face smoothed and her hair darkened as signs of her false age disappeared. Slowly, she straightened to her full height before the light faded away once more. But not from her eyes. The glow remained there as she studied me, her face flushed with anger.

I didn't consciously make my choice before words tumbled from my mouth in a rush.

"I didn't mean to kill Hugh, and I swear never to touch your mirror again. I vow I'll be a proper young lady. Please, Mama. I'll do as you ask if only you allow me to eat."

Her gaze narrowed on me, and my stomach took that moment to growl loudly. She looked at Porcia then Cecilia.

"Come with me," she said.

She strode from the room without another glance in my direction.

As soon the door closed behind Porcia, I exhaled slowly and looked around me. Blame could still be cast my direction if Maeve thought for a moment I'd escaped my bond. She would need proof that I hadn't. Pretending ignorance about any knowledge of the mirror's destruction wouldn't be enough.